A PARROT SPEAKS TO A BUSINESS TYCOON

A. SENTHIVEL

INDIA • SINGAPORE • MALAYSIA

ISBN 979-8-88591-685-1

Contents

1. A Modern Midas

'$50 billion deal! I am just invincible. Whatever I lay my hands upon, just turns gold!', Mr. Naughtisome prided himself, as he was walking into his 100 floor house, over the deal that he just clinched by defeating a dozen other companies that were competing to get this opportunity to supply the core processors for a leading Note Pads manufacturing company! Naughtisome is lovingly called Mr. Naught by the people who are close to him. In the twenty-five years of his business life, he has hardly let go of any tender or business deal. For him, it is not business. It is his self-image. Mr. Naught is synonymous with success!

Naught's father had left behind a small garment manufacturing unit and his father's death coincided with Naught's final year in the college. With a degree in Commerce and a business unit waiting to be taken over, Mr. Naught had very little time to think of enjoying his life in any manner as would guys do in their youth. No pubs, no bars, no dating girls! His enjoyment ended the day he stepped out of college. Naught's own high regard for his father and survival pressures compelled him to take up the languishing business and spruce it up to shining glory.

‘You look tired Naught; will you have some fresh juice…?’ his loving wife walked towards him and assisted him in removing his overcoat.

‘I thought I looked victorious today. I just did my magic once again! The most leading Notepads in the world will be powered by the processor that I am going to supply. I don’t know why God has chosen me particularly to bestow all the talents of the world!’ quipped Mr. Naught in great self-admiration.

‘You said you might not turn up for lunch today. So, I have not prepared the elaborate menu that you usually go for. Should we fly out to the Radisson for lunch?’, said Mrs. Ruby Naught.

‘Should we go out? I thought we are getting past lunch time’.

‘In no time we can be on the Radisson’s roof. We just have to push the dedicated elevator button and there we are at our 100th floor and I have lined up three choppers for this week. By the way, did you see that new 12-seater chopper that you ordered 4 months ago?’ said Mrs. Ruby with a sense of pride over-whelming her while thinking of her husband’s nonchalant style in which he orders big things as if they were children’s toys!

‘Alright, we will go for the first ride on that chopper and after lunch we will go to our private airstrip and take the new Boeing 15-seater jet and finish our social visit to

Mr. Andersons. Otherwise, your father will not spare us! Your father loves his younger brother so much! I think it is about 2 hours flight from here to Mr. Anderson's place. The cozy lounge in that new Boeing should give me the much-needed rest so that I can think of my next conquest in the war of business.

Mrs. Ruby and Mr. Naught walked out of the Radisson after a hearty meal. And there was a surprise call and Mr. Naught had to return to his office to meet his counterpart from London who happened to be in the city on some personal work. Mr. Naught had a flair for catching up with people and he air-dashed to his office and finished his short meeting with his guest. And it was still only 3 pm. He postponed his social visit and returned home.

He thought he would just go to the 20th floor and plunge into the lukewarm pool that would comfort his frazzled nerves. Six floors of his house had six different swimming pools with different gradation in temperatures. Mr. Naught was not even willing to give the time needed to adjust the temperatures of the pool. So, he decided, he would have six different pools on six different floors, two earmarked for children! But again, it was a long time since a he took a stroll in the sprawling 20-acre garden cum orchard that he had created at the back of his 100-floor house. Mr. Naught spent a fortune in creating this lush green garden. Not that the plants cost him a bomb. But the land. He had a prolonged negotiation with owners of the houses that were earlier occupying the current garden and he paid them up to 10 times more market value in order to acquire this space for his favorite garden.

Now the garden has a variety of flowers, an orchard and patches of wild growth of plants. And a lot of pet animals lived happily there. And the orchard was blooming with varieties of fruits including avocado, cherry, papaya, fig, apple and grape, and no wonder this became a place of feast for a variety of different birds! Mr. Naught sometimes spotted even migratory birds perch on the high branches – yellow billed cuckoos, black-throated green warblers and red-tailed hawks are his favorite sight! Mr. Naught kept some meat in the garden especially for the predator hawks and falcons! A few times he lost his favorite bunnies to these hawks. So passionate about birds was Mr. Naught that sometimes people around him wondered if he was a businessman or an ornithologist!

Mr. Naught walked into the garden and he sat on his favorite reclining sofa with his legs perched atop a stool meant for that purpose, under the cool shade of the pipal tree, whose seeds Mr. Naught had brought from India with a lot of penchant that he usually shows towards tree varieties! It was a hot day out there and sitting here under the tree was more pleasurable than sitting in a room blasting with powerful air-conditioners! As he was ensconced in his super-comfy sofa, the gentle breeze that was blowing wiped off all the day-to-day pressures of his hectic business life. He enjoyed the breeze and was relaxing. But then the thoughts were, as usual, running from New York to Australia, covering all his business set-ups across the globe. He thought to himself, 'Miles to go before I sleep!'. Another thought swirled across his ever-avaricious mind, `Before I die, I should have become the world's richest person, exceeding the second position at least by ten times'.

Again, one more thought twirled into his go-getter mind, 'More than 90% of the world businesses should be mine…'

`No', a strange voice was heard!

Mr. Naught was startled to hear this voice from nowhere and he looked around in bewilderment. He thought that it must have been his own imagination. But then why a 'no' to my fiercest ambition, he wondered! Two minutes passed in silence except for the gentle rustle and whistle of the air caressing the leaves of the trees. After a while, Mr. Naught's attention came back to his own thoughts and the same thought was running again, `More than 90% of the world's businesses should be mine….'

'No, no' the voice was heard again from up the pipal tree, but the voice was shriller this time. Mr. Naught was now sure it was not his imagination. He sensed someone or something was around!

Perplexed and curious to figure out what is happening, Mr. Naught gently raised his head and looked in the direction from where he thought the voice came but didn't see anyone up there.

He became a little disturbed. It looked like someone definitely spoke this time. He just reached out to his pocket gun just in case there was anyone really out there!

He slowly settled again into the easy chair and this time it took some time for him to come back and continue with his thoughts. `Life is all about my winning', a thought swept across his mind.

'No, no, no…!', a distinct and stern voice spoke this time.

2. A New Voice from Nowhere

With his heart beat increasing and a little adrenaline pumping, Mr. Naught this time looked up and started scanning the entire tree to see if anyone was hiding there. For he was convinced this time that the voice definitely came from up the pipal tree. To his surprise, he saw only a parrot sitting on a branch and eating something. He just ignored the parrot and he did not imagine any reason to link the parrot with the 'no, no, no' voice.

Mr. Naught was a little confused. 'Why am I imagining voices, that too, negative answers to my thoughts?', he was breaking his head!

'You are not imagining, Mr. Naught, you are listening to me, *me* the parrot' came a clear human-like voice from up the tree. Mr. Naught was taken aback and he looked up at the parrot and said, 'Was that you who spoke'?

'Yes, I did', pat came the reply!

Mr. Naught couldn't believe his eyes and rubbed both his eyes and glared at the parrot again. There it was staring at him but at the same time eating some fruit. Mr. Naught leaned back and slowly adjusted the reclining sofa in such a way that he could face the parrot effortlessly. His head was reeling in disbelief!

With a lot of irritation, Mr. Naught asked the parrot, 'How dare you gainsay my victory thoughts?'

'Truth' retorted the parrot.

Mr. Naught got highly annoyed and said, 'What nonsense? What truth do you know about my life?'

'I know the whole truth about your life,' said the parrot, not heeding the perplexed state of Mr. Naught.

Mr. Naught couldn't believe his own eyes and ears. The parrot seemed to be talking flawlessly and the voice was almost human-like!

'You are saying you know the entire truth about my life. Can you mention one truth about my business life,' Mr. Naught said to the parrot with skepticism filled to the brim. `Let me see what this little creature is talking about', he thought to himself.

'You have spent $15 billion only on bribe paid out to different government officials and representatives from other companies in order to get your deals worth $125 billion in the last one year, haven't you, Mr. Naught?' said the parrot in a matter-of-fact voice.

'What, $15 billion on bribes? Impossible!' came a weak reply from Mr. Naught. He seemed to know that the figure cited by the parrot was close to truth. He became uncomfortable and started squirming in his easy chair. 'How the hell does this parrot know what happened in my life, what are the chances that this parrot might not leak all this to newspapers!', Mr. Naught started racking his brain.

To confirm that this parrot knows more, he asked one more question – 'Okay, I accept that I spent $15 billion on bribes. But do you have information on how many top employees I have poached from other organizations?'

'Seventy percent of your top managers are poached from other companies. You are a shrewd businessman. You don't believe in loyalties or ethics. Whenever you met top managers from other companies on business, you never hesitated to play the dirty game of hijacking them to your company within a month or two! You first hired Mr. Nixon from that mining company and later engineered your own shrewd ways to buy out that company itself.'

Mr. Naught was startled to hear the graphic details about his dealings. 'Is he a parrot or is he a technologically advanced robot sent by my business enemies to spy on me?' wondered a rattled Mr. Naught.

He pulled out his pocket gun and pointed at the parrot and shouted, 'Who are you? Are you really a parrot? Or are you a machine?'

No sooner did Mr. Naught finish his sentence than a drop of poop fell next to him on the ground. Mr. Naught could see that this was really the poop of a live bird. And this confirmed that the parrot was really a biological being, and not a robot!

Seeing the helpless situation in which Mr. Naught found himself, the parrot started laughing loudly, 'You helpless guy. Is gun ever the answer? Can't you speak to me and find out if I am a bird or a robot. Why are you experiencing this insecurity and fear? Unless you have walked the wrong path, where is the need for you to feel so insecure?'

'You are talking too much Mr. Parrot', came the angry response from Mr. Naught.

'Truth' said the parrot again in the same nonchalant manner. 'I am a Ms. Parrot, for your information,' the parrot added.

Mr. Naught could not control his anger and shouted, 'What the heck are you talking about? What is truth? How do you know I am pursuing the wrong path? I have worked my ass off and have built a business empire worth $200 billion. I have given employment to thousands of people. I am an ambitious man. Don't ever dare say I walk the wrong path' warned Mr. Naught.

'But then why can't you make this point calmly that you are not walking the wrong path? Why so much of agitation and anger? Why are you so flustered? Isn't there some truth hiding behind your disturbance?' said the parrot with the calmness of a cool philosopher. 'Don't you have enough control over you to speak to me in a cool manner?' the parrot spoke in a toned-down voice.

'I can...but, somehow, I grew angry hearing you say I walk the wrong path. I don't walk the wrong path completely. Occasionally, in order to close my business deals, I do deviate from healthy business norms. But then, out there, people are not straightforward, either. Things don't happen if I don't bribe them or extend to them some favors. If all of them were perfect, I would also be straightforward and perfect. Do you want me to lose my business deals in the name of being honest? Why don't you go from door to door and tell them to be honest?' said Mr. Naught in a highly irritated voice.

'My concern is you. I am now talking to *you*. I am now talking only about you. Will you please talk only about yourself? Otherwise, I will not talk to you. I have better business to do', the parrot said.

Mr. Naught was not fully reconciled to this reality of being in a conversation with a parrot, yet! He was wondering what would happen if he shared this weird experience with his friends! They might roll on the floor laughing, he thought. But he was curious enough to continue.

'What a rude parrot! But this parrot seems to know things intuitively. Let me not lose this opportunity; let me also understand what the parrot thinks about my future plans and ambitions. This parrot could possess some powers of predictions. I will cajole this parrot into talking about my future too,' Mr. Naught thought to himself.

'You can ask me directly, you don't have to fool me or cajole me,' said the parrot.

'Oh, this parrot reads my mind, it is very dangerous. He can spill the beans about my activities to others. Let me finish her off.' Mr. Naught pulled his gun out and looked up to shoot the parrot. But lo, the parrot was missing!

Mr. Naught heaved a sigh of relief that the troublesome parrot had flown away! Mr. Naught started relaxing and started feeling relieved. 'Hell with this parrot', he thought.

A few minutes passed in silence.

'I am here only, Mr. Naught, I am not gone! I am in the very same place where I was before. Come on shoot me.', said the parrot.

Mr. Naught could hear the voice of the parrot from around the same place where she was sitting but couldn't see her there!

3. The Parrot Urges Self-Mastery

Mr. Naught's thoughts started running wild. 'This parrot has the capacity to disappear from human eyes but still be present there. She doesn't know what great shooting skills I have. I will finish her off the moment I see her', Mr. Naught decided this time firmly.

'I thought some amount of humanity will be still left with you. You have become an automaton. You are behaving like a pre-programmed robot! You have no friendly feelings or fellow feelings. You seem to abhor truth and disdain people who speak truth. Why don't you negotiate instead of resorting to your gun? If gun were the only solution, all of us would have become extinct by now! Why don't you have some Self-mastery and run your mind with some control instead of allowing your reaction mechanisms to rule you over?' said the parrot in an authoritative voice.

N: 'What is this arrogant long lecture? What do you know about Self-mastery?', shouted Mr. Naught in an uncontrollable fashion.

P: Pretty opposite of what you know!

N: What do you mean?

P: What do you mean by Self-mastery?

N: Gaining mastery over one's self – body and mind.

P: Is it all?

N: Yes, one should have control over one's body and one's mind. And one should be careful about what one eats, whether he works out in the gym properly on a daily basis or not, and if he has control over his thoughts and behavior. This is Self-mastery. But you said what you knew about Self-mastery was the opposite of what I knew. To turn logic upside down, you must be nuts…

P: You are scripted in 'I am right, you are wrong' and so *you* must be nuts…

N: (Waving his gun again) Don't dare cross your limits, after all you are a creature, inferior to mankind.

P: Mr. Naught, truth can come from anywhere, anybody. Even if a stone were to utter the truth, you should have the humility and intelligence to accept it. Otherwise, you don't deserve the tag, 'human'.

N: Fine...enough of your sermon!

Mr. Naught hides his feelings of defeat by acting as if he were cleaning the surface of the gun with his hand kerchief. 'Now, tell me what you mean by Self-mastery.'

P: Self-mastery does not mean you master the Self. You simply work towards a situation where you allow the Self to master the rest of you!

N: What do you mean? You are confusing me.

P: The Self inside you is in a sleep mode right now. What is dominant in you right now is your peripherality, yes, your body and mind. Instead of the body and mind being dominant, you should work towards creating a condition within you where the Self can blossom.

N: How do I do it? How do I help the Self blossom?

P: Help the body and mind be in quietude. When the body and mind diminish their activity levels, the Self will surface.

N: How?

P: By sitting as an observer of your own body and mind, by sitting in non-meditation.

N: What non-sense? I have heard of 'meditation'. What is this `non-meditation' you are talking about? Are you mentally imbalanced, Ms. Parrot?

P: Don't be impetuous. At every point and every turn, don't try to prove that you know better. Odds are that you don't!

N: Ok, enough of preaching! Now, tell me about sitting in non-meditation.

Mr. Naught thought if he were not careful, this parrot could drive him mad! And he was ready to listen to the parrot carefully with a critical mind so that he could defeat the parrot and chase her off!

N: Now, speak!

P: Okay, sit erect and close your eyes!

N: Sitting erect is okay. But I will not close my eyes.

P: Why?

N: I will not, don't ask me why, I am not comfortable with that idea.

P: What a coward you are!

N: Don't insult me by saying I am a coward. I am daring. Didn't you see me carrying a gun?

P: That's why I called you a coward.

N: I think you are going over-board. Don't push me beyond the limits of my tolerance.

P: Who sets the limits to your tolerance?

N: Okay. I accept. I can have more tolerance than I think I have.

Mr. Naught slowly develops a vague feeling that his conversation with the parrot might turn out to be an eye-opener in some way. So, he decides to control his ways with the parrot!

N: I will close my eyes on condition that you do not do anything harmful to me.

P: You are 200 pounds and what is my weight! What harm can I do to you? And I don't wield a gun….!

N: Still…

Mr. Naught agrees to listen to the parrot. And he closes his eyes.

N: Now, I have closed my eyes. What next?

P: Next one hour is non-existent, you imagine. I will call out your name after exactly one hour and instruct you about the next step!

With impatience Mr. Naught opens his eyes and frowns at the Parrot straight!

N: What bullshit is it? You said you would guide me to get into non-meditation. Now, you are saying you will tell me about it after one hour. And you want me to sit for one hour closing my eyes but you are not saying what I will do during that one hour! Are you crazy? Are you in your senses?

P: Will you please switch off your judgement-mode for some time? At least for the next one or two hours!

You are becoming helplessly reactive to everything! If you show patience, I will explain how you can get into non-mediation. Otherwise, I will go. My friends will be waiting for me.

N: Oh, you have friends, too? Poor fellows…I wish they got some better friend…!

P: Once again you are sarcastic. See you good bye.

The parrot started flapping her wings as if she was ready to depart.

N: Oh, my dear, come on, I was only joking. I know you are intelligent. Otherwise, I wouldn't be wasting my time...!

P: Again judgmental! You think no end of yourself, Mr. Naught! Anyway, there seems to be some amount of good sense in you and I respect that. I will tell you about non-meditation. If you have observed, the phrase, 'to meditate upon' means 'to think of or concentrate on something'. It means that we should focus on any one thing with all our attention. So, in the light of this meaning, 'meditation' would signify being focused on something, some object or some thought. Do you agree with me?

N: Yes, go ahead and tell me what is it that you are trying to say.

P: I am saying sit there and '*non-meditate*'.

N: Is it possible? What do I do with those train of thoughts that surface to my awareness?

P: Non-mediate on them. Just sit and ignore thoughts instead of trying to complete them or build upon them. Sit for five minutes and then we shall continue. Is that acceptable to you? Now I am not asking you to sit for one hour, just for 5 minutes!

4. Why is Non-Meditation Such a Struggle?

Mr. Naught closed his eyes. And even after 5 minutes, he did not open his eyes. The parrot thought high of him that this man, although, fresh to non-meditation, is proving to be very promising. But then, ten minutes passed and Mr. Naught did not show any signs of opening his eyes. His body started slowly swaying towards either left or right. The parrot had a doubt and in order to confirm that doubt, she slanted her head and started focusing on some sound that was coming from Mr. Naught. To her surprise, the parrot realized that Mr. Naught had fallen asleep and had started snoring! Peeved off at this sight, the parrot called out his name loud enough to wake him up…

P: Mr. Naught, did you fall asleep?

Mr. Naught woke up with a start and rubbed his eyes.

N: It looks like. I tried to sit in non-meditation but then I am not sure what happened! Don't you think I have been in non-meditation?

P: Mr. Naught, stop being funny! You have not been in non-meditation. You have been in non-mindfulness. You have been non-serious. I will see you later… you had better continue with your sleep.

The parrot acted as if she was annoyed.

N: No, no, dear Ms. Parrot, I am sorry. Don't be so serious. We will continue. Now tell me what to do...!

The parrot couldn't tell him why she chose to speak to him voluntarily. She had her own reasons. She was not willing to disclose anything till she fulfilled the purpose of meeting him. But then, to deal with a puffed-up man like Mr. Naught was somewhat a challenging job for her!

P: Close your eyes, be wary not to sleep off and sit in non-meditation for 5 minutes…

Mr. Naught again closes his eyes and sits erect. This time around, the body was sitting straight and erect, no left or right motion. Five minutes passed; ten minutes passed….! The parrot was proud that her role as a guru was so successful!

P: Mr. Naught, open your eyes, and tell me about your experiences…

N: Hurrah! I have given clearance to two of my major upcoming real estate projects of a mega scale...! I didn't do it consciously, the thoughts spun themselves out! In fact, I had not set aside enough conscious time to think about the different aspects of these upcoming projects...dear Ms. Parrot, I think non-meditation really helps....!

P: You are wrong Mr. Naught! What helped you just now was your meditation and not non-meditation.

N: What do you mean?

P: I had explained that if you focus on one thought, it becomes meditation. If you don't follow any thought at all, that is non-meditation!

N: But then, what will I be aware of if I don't entertain any thought at all? Will there not be 'nothing' to experience? Don't we need something to be in awareness of?

P: That is the difference between meditation and non-meditation. Only if you practice non-meditation will you ever create that situation conducive for the Self to surface! Only then Self-mastery will happen!

N: This is strange. The whole world is talking about the importance of meditation. You are talking about non-meditation. If you don't entertain any thought at all, will I not become mad out of emptiness?

P: No, you will not. Rather you will reverse your current madness if you sat in non-meditation.

N: Are you hinting that I am mad right now? How dare you?

P: No, no, what I meant is that even if you were to be in madness right now, it will get reversed if you sat in non-meditation. Now, tell me if you can sit in non-meditation for the next 30 minutes. Will you try?

N: Okay I will try. But will you stay back till then?

P: Sure, I will.

Mr. Naught closes his eyes. It is almost forty minutes when he reopens his eyes.

P: Mr. Naught, tell me what you experienced.

N: I was dead.

P: How can a dead person come alive? Are you joking?

N: No, no, for some time, the thoughts were running riot. I became aware of your instruction that I should behave as if I had nothing to do with my body and mind and I continued to sit without expecting to do any mental work at all!

P: Good, and then...?

N: And then, some fleeting awareness came to my mind to the effect quite some time had passed in between…

P: That's good, Mr. Naught. You seem to be a good learner!

N: Oh, you know how to appreciate people, too! I thought you were like one of those bad HR managers who always found fault with others.

P: With a hard nut like you, unless I am firm…

N: Stop that non-sense, simply because you possess knowledge about higher truths, you cannot talk down to me…

P: Okay, I am sorry if you think I was talking down to you.

N: Oh, you have humility, too...!

P: Humility is my default state.

N: Okay, let us proceed. Now that I have done thirty minutes of non-meditation! Does this mean I too have Self-mastery?

P: Far from it.

N: Don't irritate me. Why did you waste my time? You know I value time. Every one hour in my business means quite a few million dollars.

P: That's in business life. This is not business life. This is life, pure life.

N: You mean to say business is not life?

P: No, business alone is not life. Life includes business, business does not include life.

N: That's why I am a human being, and you are just a parrot! You just cannot appreciate the value of doing business and amassing wealth!

P: Comparison is odious. Have you forgotten this simple lesson taught to you in your school? My point was that you can have this time vs money calculations only with respect to your business. Not here where you are trying to acquire Self-mastery! Self-mastery is your Self acquiring mastery over all your peripheral aspects of life, your body, emotions and mind. For the Self to emerge dominant, you need to practice non-meditation, for hours and hours.

N: If you can't quantify the number of hours, you had better not open your mouth! You don't deserve talking to a business tycoon like me if you can't have some sense of arithmetic.

P: I do have a sense of arithmetic. But you will be pissed off if I mention that.

N: I am an open-minded person. And I think scientifically. Don't think I am a silly fool…

P: For you to acquire that Self-mastery, it will take a few lifetimes.

N: What? A few lifetimes? It is rubbish. Don't you know the powerful norm in business life that any colossal task can be done within a short while if you divide the task among people and get it done through the delegation route?

P: This logic of yours proves once again that you need lifetimes in order to acquire Self-mastery!

Mr. Naught became wild hearing the sarcastic remark. He controlled the movement of his right hand that wanted to pull out his gun. In spite of his anger, he wanted to understand why the parrot made this remark.

N: Tell me why, why the heck did you say that I would take lifetimes to acquire Self-mastery?

P: See, anything else can be delegated. Can you delegate eating food? Can you delegate the answering of nature's calls? The same way, Self-mastery cannot be delegated. I can only help you by encouraging you to sit for a greater number of hours in non-meditation. But I cannot do it on your behalf.

N: Are you sure, I believe nothing is impossible. There must be a short-cut.

P: Please don't bring the over-smart and cunning ways of your business style into the domain of Self-mastery!

N: See, don't you dare pass rude comments about my business style! The whole world admires me for my business-savvy disposition.

P: Business is both your strength and weakness. Your hunger for more business and more money has kept your thought process always in the boil. Business aspirations have not allowed you even one moment of peace in your life. Of course, I do understand that very huge money is at stake! Your business empire needs your constant attention. You need to take care of them, nurture them.

Otherwise, they will collapse, triggering a chain reaction which will impact your reputation and destiny. But, in order to safeguard your interests, you have subscribed to even immoral and illegal ways which your own conscience does not accept!

N: Don't talk as if you have been a witness to all the happenings in my life.

P: Yes, I have been.

N: What do you mean? You say I have resorted to immoral ways. Can you point out any one instance in my life where I have been immoral?

5. Sexual Escapades of Mr. Naught

P: That day, when you decided to go to Sydney, you charted a flight with four bedrooms. Though two of your own aircraft were available, you did not take them because they only had two bed rooms each. So, you hired this ultra-luxury airliner with four bedrooms and you did so with a master plan. Two were given to your executives. You reserved the bedroom next to you for a lady business associate and guest. All others took your word for it. And you know what you did with that lady in her room in the name of business discussions…should I elaborate on it?

N: (Mr. Naught was shocked to hear this!) No, no, but tell me how did you know all this…?

Mr. Naught became a little nervous and uncomfortable as there was a chance his wife could walk into the garden anytime! In resentment, Mr. Naught switched to his characteristic business style now.

N: See, tell me what you want as a quid pro quo. I will do anything for you! Do you want a separate orchard for you, your family and friends? I will buy one for you. But, please, this information should not be leaked out at all. I have a wonderful wife, beautiful children and a harmonious family. If ever my wife comes to know, it will destroy the very foundation of my life. Without peace of mind, I cannot do business. Please. Tell me your price for keeping this a secret.

The parrot continued as if his request fell on deaf ears!

P: And in the very same trip, your mind wavered and you were after a beautiful hostess in the Marriott hotel in Sydney. The girl tried to explain hard that it is against her work ethic to get close to a guest. But you were hell bent on a date with her. But then you found the accompanying guest a hindrance and decided to send her back within two hours of arrival at Sydney. And the guest-lady couldn't understand your strange behavior. And the hostess in the Marriott hotel decided to bring the matter to the notice of her seniors....

N: Enough, enough of this! Please stop! Dear Ms. Parrot, you had better go away. I thought I would learn something higher from you. But you are digging out the worst fears and memories from inside me...

P: Why do you worry? I was only pointing out some instances as you had asked for it. I am not here to extract favors or deals from you! You can take it from me I am your friend. I will not let you down...!

On hearing this, his heartbeat started de-escalating and he slowly became composed. Mr. Naught had a big sigh of relief.

N: Now, you have this power of mind-reading, tell me how you developed this skill. If only I had this power of mind-reading, I would just buy off the entire planet!

P: That's why that power is not given to you!

N: What do you mean?

P: Yes, when you are too full of yourself, you will destroy others if you possessed higher powers of mind-reading, clairvoyance or telepathy. Such powers are born when selfishness is dead!

N: When selfishness is dead, why do we need these powers?

P: When your selfish desires are dead, you become a true human being who cares for the well-being of all. When you become such a compassionate human being, these powers are a part of you. Not that you depend on them, but they are there as a part and parcel of your life. When you experience yourself as the whole existence, even if such powers were vested in you, you would not use them against anyone because you would be in the knowing that all is One – everybody and everything is a part of you!

N: Okay, let it be so. Now, promise me you will not talk about my affairs to my wife.

Mr. Naught was not in a frame of mind to appreciate the higher truths the parrot was talking about.

P: I am here to open your eyes to your own inconsistencies and vagaries. I will not let you down, I promise. And last year, when you visited Thailand's capital Bangkok....

N: I know what I did. I fell in love, temporarily, with a girl in the spa. And I had extended my stay for two more weeks in order to steal some more time with the girl. Recently, she visited me in New York and she still hopes that I will accept her as a live-in, if not as a wife! For Heaven's sake will you please stop this list...?

P: Is it embarrassing?

N: It is not embarrassing. But I feel uncomfortable thinking about those episodes.

P: When you yourself chose to involve yourself with those girls with a great amount of fondness, why should you feel uncomfortable?

Mr. Naught was in a fix, not knowing what to say!

P: Why are you silent?

N: No...my wife... she trusts me.

P: So what!

N: I should not violate trust if I expect the same from her.

P: Who said so? Is there a written rule that you should not betray your wife?

N: Can you always live life by written rule? Isn't there such a thing as feeling good or feeling bad?

P: Oh, is this Mr. Naught speaking or somebody else! I can't believe my own ears!

6. Let Me Listen Hard...What do you Think about Sex?

Mr. Naught, by this time, is convinced that this Parrot is all-knowing and it can read others' minds! So, Mr. Naught now decides to clarify all the doubts relating to the other aspects of his life, too.

N: Don't be sarcastic. Rather appreciate me that I have some conscience operating inside me.

P: Is there anyone in this world who does not have his conscience in operation? Everyone's conscience is fully operational, all the time. But how many of them stop to listen to it? One needs to cultivate the habit of connecting with one's conscience daily! Otherwise, one will always remain unconnected to one's conscience.

N: Now tell me, you seem to know through your extra-sensory perception things that human beings normally don't know. I have some questions and will you answer them straight?

P: Sure, I will.

N: Tell me why this constant attraction towards the opposite sex is there in me! This attraction is operating all the time in me. Not that I want to play with the lives of girls, but there is a constant desire to be in the company of girls, I hope you understand what I mean…

P: Yes, yes, I understand this urge very well. No voluptuous girl has escaped your attention. And your heart stops if you see a buxom woman!

N: Is it a bad urge?

P: Don't you know the answer?

N: I really don't know. And I feel bad that I have this urge!

P: Why should you feel bad?

N: Because I think it is bad to love so many women.

P: There is nothing wrong!

N: What!

'This parrot must be immoral too', thought Mr. Naught!

P: I meant there is nothing wrong with the urge to seek the opposite sex.

N: You mean to say I can continue with my extra-marital affairs?

P: No and yes!

N: Why are you confusing me? Why don't you give the answer without beating about the bush?

P: The sexual urge is needed for your species to continue, or for that matter, even for our species to continue! But you must understand the basic function and purpose of sex.

N: Isn't sex the sum and substance of pleasure?

P: You perverted guy! How can pleasure be the basic purpose of sex?

N: I thought so. Why else do men and women seek sex so much, day in and day out?

P: The sexual desire is the built-in, unconscious drive every member of your species has in him or her. The drive is nature's way of making sure you guys procreate and continue the chain of human existence. Without that desire to unite with the opposite sex, how will procreation happen?

N: So, do you mean to say sex is only for procreation and not for pleasure?

P: I did not say that.

N: What else do I understand from your statement?

P: The primary purpose of sex is procreation. Pleasure is incidental.

N: Should we then avoid sex for pleasure?

P: My point is that it is futile to entertain sexual desire beyond its purpose.

N: You are again saying that I should not indulge in sex for the sake of pleasure! In my life, procreation is over. Does that mean I should not have sex at all, even with my wife?

P: I only said it is futile to entertain sexual desire beyond its purpose. There is no end to this desire. Be aware that this desire keeps tantalizing you. Whenever sexual desire surfaces, become aware that the basic purpose of sex is only procreation and that this desire is redundant. Every time the desire surfaces, you don't have to seek a partner.

N: Will it not become an unfulfilled desire? Should I suppress my desires?

P: This desire, in its very nature, is unfulfillable! The craving to unite with the opposite sex is un-ending. Can you physically unite with the opposite sex round the clock, round the year, as if you had nothing else to do in life?

N: What is your conclusion about sex, then?

P: It is up to you.

N: Isn't there an objective norm as to how much of sex one should indulge in?

P: Each is the norm-maker, depending upon his or her needs.

Mr. Naught starts wondering if he was not wasting his time with the parrot as the parrot seemed to mystify things although it clarified certain other things! May be the parrot is not adept at decision-making, Mr. Naught wondered!

N: Okay I understand my needs and I will go accordingly. Are you sure it is my right to go about fulfilling my desires?

P: Absolutely. But on one condition!

N: What is this rider?

P: You are free to go about fulfilling your desires provided you acknowledge your wife's freedom, too!

N: To do what?

P: To fulfil her own sexual desires, if she had any.

Mr. Naught got wild at this and picked up a stone in rage to throw at the parrot! I will kill you right here if you speak non-sense! How dare you suggest my wife stray, too?

P: Do unto others what you would have them do unto you, you must have read this in your school, haven't you?

N: Don't sermon me. I know better. Men are privileged to go astray but not women.

P: Which law says this?

N: It is an established way of life. Straying has always been men's privilege, never that of women!

P: Is there a scientific basis to this traditional thinking?

N: ....yes....no......yes, yes...

P: What? Be unequivocal Mr. Naught!

N: Historically, men have been the bread winners and they have taken the hardships of going round amidst dangers and they have risked their own lives in order to save their wives and children. So, in this hardship drama, it is okay for men to taste a little bit of happiness by indulging in a little extra sex. What is wrong?

P: Did men do a favor to their wife and children by earning the bread and by offering protection to them?

Mr. Naught starts scratching his head in thinking. He finds his logic untenable.

N: No. It is his duty, and it is in his interest to take care of his own family members.

P: Then, how is this privilege of straying justified for men?

N: So, your conclusion is that I can have my freedom to stray if I reciprocally give that freedom to my wife, too. Isn't it?

P: You cannot give her that freedom.

N: Then?

P: You can only acknowledge.

N: This is too much! I had better stay loyal only to my wife. What the heck! Giving freedom to my wife to stray!.... What non-sense!

P: Do unto others...

N: Enough, enough, tell me this why do men and women indulge in homosexuality if procreation is the basic purpose of sex? Aren't you wrong in your understanding?

Mr. Naught thought he proved himself to be smarter than the parrot and was patting his back with pride!

P: Sex is for procreation.

N: Stop your non-sense. Do you mean to say all those people who indulge in homosexuality are ignorant?

P: It is their choice.

N: You better answer my question without prevaricating! Are they ignorant?

P: Sex is for procreation. And this serves as the reference point for anybody to correct his or her thinking.

N: Do you mean to say they are wasting their time indulging in homosexuality?

P: No comments! Everybody has a right to make their choices in life.

7. Transcending Sexuality

The Parrot continued, `your species, i.e., mankind is reputed for leading life in a progressive manner. Humans always attach value to meaning. Humans usually abhor meaningless activities. This is because humans are the most intelligent species on this planet. But, when pleasure preponderates in one's mind, the truth about sex is forgotten and when truth is forgotten, distorted ways are born.'

N: Since so many people choose to practice homosexuality, it must be an intelligent choice, too! Don't you think so?

P: Exception to rule is also a rule.

N: So, meaningless pursuits are also a part of life?

P: The supreme spirit of humans is to correct their course of action even if deviations have already happened! It is this indomitable and persistent desire to lead meaningful lives that marks the humans as an advanced species. But the human mind is error-prone, too. While it does so many good things, it can go wrong, too. Sometimes the human thought can become its own justification, without being supported by truth! Unvalidated thoughts should be invalidated.

N: Why should human thoughts be validated by a reference to truth?

P: A few individuals carrying on with unvalidated thoughts becomes a scourge in society over a period of time! Society is intertwined and inter-connected. Influences do spill over. The young of your species learn things by copying and by imitating. So, it is the responsibility of the grown-up to set up healthy examples for the young to follow.

N: Why care about the young? Is it not the individual's top-most priority to live life whichever way he or she wants?

P: You have picked up many things from your elders, haven't you? The total social environment in which you grew up had a big influence on your thought and behavior patterns! If the environment had been highly sordid, you would have been a corrupted child, too. Your psychological scripting rules you over, like it or not!

N: So…

P: It is the duty of the elders to validate their thoughts and behavior by a reference to truth.

N: If we ignore this?

P: Every individual has to pay his debts. As you sow, so shall you reap, too. Things will catch up. First of all, one's own inner man will screw him or her up. Unvalidated thoughts and actions have a way of catching up! On death bed, no individual can escape the harsh reprimands of the inner man.

N: Are you a teacher of morality?

P: I am a teacher of reality!

N: Okay, you talk big! How will anyone validate one's own thoughts?

P: The easiest way is to listen to the inner voice every now and then. The inner voice is the voice of wisdom and the resultant of the integration of all one's experiences, knowledge and one's own unique inborn nature. Any given time, the inner voice is your highest guidance!

Mr. Naught was disturbed now. He had so far been indifferent to his inner voice! Now, his inner voice has started surfacing! He wanted to move to the next question and the parrot, he thought, would shake him further if he continued the discussions on this topic.

N: What is your enlightened view on homosexuality, finally?

P: See, transcending sex impulse is a sign of a mature soul. Transcending hetero sexuality is a great accomplishment from the spiritual standpoint. But, after transcending hetero-sexual impulses, if people do not know what to do with their life, they might turn to homosexuality. In a way, it can be interpreted that homosexuals are people who have transcended sexuality, in the first place. They are in a way the most suitable people to turn inward and seek their true home.

N: What do you mean by true home?

P: By home I mean their deepest inner nature. It is their spiritual nature. Not knowing what they are seeking, they get into a distorted mode.

N: Homosexuals will sue you for a huge compensation if they hear your words.

P: What will they get in return? I can give them a few fruits. That's all! What do I own? Anyway, if they had the larger picture of life in their mind, they would only become curious to know what I mean by seeking their home.

N: You are mystifying the subject.

P: My job is to demystify.

'Arrogant and conceited parrot', Mr. Naught thought to himself. He did not want to articulate because the Parrot could drag him into another endless argument.

N: Now, tell me what you mean by seeking one's home. What is the process involved?

P: Don't you know? Why feign ignorance!

N: No, I am not acting as if I did not know. Seriously. Please throw some light.

P: A human being is not just the body-mind complex. There is a deeper reality to man. He is fundamentally an unlimited, omniscient spirit. In other words, he or she is fundamentally the Self, pure existence, pure consciousness and pure bliss. When a man tries to know his true nature through non-meditation, he slowly reaches a point where he clearly sees a distinction between his body-mind and his true nature, the Self. When he realizes his Self, he transcends all physicality, hetero or homosexuality. The Self is without any attributes. But it tends to take on itself the qualities of the object it shines upon, I mean the body. This is a sort of hypnotization! And most of humanity lives in this hypnotized state! And all you need to do is de-hypnotize yourself through non-meditation!

N: Confusing...! Do you mean to say I am not this 'Naught'?

P: No, Mr. Naught is not the *real you.* Your body is a gadget, working on borrowed power.

N: Who owns the power?

P: The Self.

N: A little too much! But tell me, how does this pursuit of seeking one's Self help one rid of homosexuality?

P: It will rid one of all sexuality, lock, stock and barrel. At the least, the compulsion will go away.

N: What is the point of it all?

P: Since you raised the question about homosexuality, I felt obliged to answer. Otherwise, it is none of my business.

N: So, you want to say that the larger picture of life includes seeking one's true nature, don't you?

P: Yes and no!

N: Addled brain! Don't you have a logical brain? Say one thing emphatically!

P: Who am I to dictate terms in a democratic world! I just shared my knowledge.

N: So, the homosexuals cannot argue their case without seeking to know their Self in the first place – is that what you are saying?

P: I don't know.

N: You have gone crazy.

Mr. Naught was tired of speaking to this Parrot! But then, he could not dismiss the arguments put forth by her. He just wanted to move on!

8. How do I Become a Global Monopoly, Ms. Parrot?

N: Okay, enough of sharing your thinking on sex. It is neither acceptable nor unacceptable. Let me ask you my next question. I want to have a monopoly over all the businesses of the world before I die. What is the likelihood?

P: As you think and act, so you become!

N: I know that! I know that! See, I inherited a small garment manufacturing firm from my father and today my business stands at $200 billion. I know I will create whatever I want to create. But…

P: I know your question.

N: Tell me, tell me, let me see if you really read my mind!

P: Your question is, "How far can I go on my business expansion?" Isn't this your question?

Mr. Naught got a little shocked because the Parrot uttered exactly the same words that he had in mind! Verbatim!

N: Why is this question coming to me? I know I am capable of organizing all that is needed to put big businesses in place – be it finance, be it the intellectual manpower or the product range. I have everything. But a question lurks inside me, and it nags me. Why is it nagging me? What is wrong in thinking of endless expansion of business?

P: Promise me you will not pull your gun out again. Only then will I tell the reason.

N: I promise.

P: You suffer from a deep sense of hollowness inside you. And you are trying to fill that hollowness with tons and tons of business desires. And, as an individual, you have crossed reasonable levels of business expansion already. Still, you are torn apart by the two sides in you – one wants to go on an expansion spree and the other just objects to it. It is that feeling of objection that you are currently experiencing but you are unable to decipher the message in words. Do you want the verbal equivalent of those feelings?

N: Yes, yes, I want to know!

P: 'Your business ambitions should reflect your desire to fulfil a certain need in society and should not be an expression of your sense of inadequacy that is raging deep inside you.'

N: Come on, business ambition is part of my identity.

P: I did not say it is not a part of your identity.

N: Then why did you say it is coming from a sense of inadequacy?

P: I am saying your very identity is flawed.

Mr. Naught is unable to control his anger. But then he has promised that he would not pull out his gun. He just bites his teeth in self-control.

N: What do you mean by saying that my identity is flawed?

P: Somewhere along the way in life, when you were just a teenager who was average in studies, not being able to have a good-looking girlfriend, yourself not-so-good-looking and lanky, not sure of your capabilities, you developed a need to prove yourself to the world! Of course, now, I must acknowledge you look handsome because of your altered self-esteem!

A sense of inadequacy was ripping you apart. The need, at that time, was more to do with proving yourself to the opposite sex. As you moved on, you wanted to get into business as you thought business would give you a lot of scope for you to improve yourself in several ways, including rich food, the budget for joining a gym, gadgets and cars to flaunt in front of girls and the money needed to spruce yourself up with the best brands of dress, shoes and perfumes! And the desire developed into a fury. And the rest of your life has simply been a pattern built on that fury! Isn't it so?

N: Let me just think...! Anyway, thank you for your compliments!

Mr. Naught goes into silence for a few minutes, recollecting the different states of mind he had experienced at different stages in his life. And he recollects how, on a certain occasion, he was saying this, in a challenging mood, to a good-looking female executive of a financial company that one day he would become the undisputed king of the business world!

N: What is wrong in this pattern of life? Yes, I felt inadequate in the initial stages and was seething inside and that is why I started working my butt off! I have worked sixteen hours every single day. But I now no longer feel that insecurity. Why talk about it?

P: Do you think you have outgrown that sense of inadequacy? Your very present still rests on the foundation of that past inadequate feeling. You always carry your past with you, don't you? When did that inadequacy leave you?

N: You mean to say I cannot undo that feeling of inadequacy?

P: You can. If you reason out and pull out that inadequate feeling, your current psychological structure will collapse. When the inner structure collapses, the outer structure will collapse, too.

N: (feels jittery) No, no, I cannot allow my outer structure to collapse. Mine is a huge business empire. And I love it.

P: But you don't seem to relish the fact that your feeling of inadequacy was the foundation stone on which your current structure is based!

N: Can I not just remove the inner aspect, not touching the outer?

P: Possible.

N: Can I do that?

P: You can. But slowly, the inner will corrode into the outer too. If you question the inner thoughts and feelings, they will definitely surface as outer manifestation, too!

N: So, according to your logic, I have some doubts about my future expansion because my inner feeling knows that I am running my business empire not solely with a desire to fulfil the society's need but to cater to my own sense of inadequacy?

P: Yes, very much. Otherwise, why will you want to get into all the businesses of the world? Why do you want a monopoly of all the businesses? What makes you think that the world will come to a stand-still if *you* stopped doing business? After all, you are only one among the 7.2 billion individuals walking on earth right now! Why should you end up doing all *their* businesses, too?

N: (gets a little irritated). Don't talk to me in that tone of voice of contempt. I can finish you off in no time, mind you.

P: You can finish me off. But you cannot finish off your inner voice!

N: Alright, you are acting too smart. Still...., you seem to talk sense. Now, tell me, what is the right perspective on business expansion?

P: Change your starting point.

N: What you mean?

P: Change the bedrock of your psychological process.

N: Don't act too smart, again. Do not speak esoteric language. I know you are trying to communicate something meaningful. But don't mystify the subject.

P: Change your foundational thought (FT).

N: Hmm............. what is that FT?

9. Foundational Thoughts

P: In your case, your FT was just an impulse to prove yourself. By any standards, now you have proved yourself. But do you feel satisfied? From nowhere, you have touched a revenue of $200 billion. Is it not, in itself, a substantial act of proving yourself?

N: Yes, it is. Companies are seen struggling to cross 50 billion and 80 billion. My capability is unique.

P: But, why do you still feel dissatisfied?

N: I don't know why. Please help me know.

P: As is the foundation stone, so is the building. The human mental mechanism is such that `if we lay one brick on top of another, there is a compulsion on the part of the mind to finish the building', says a leading thinker of your times. As your thoughts are, so is your reality!

N: What do you mean?

P: If instead of starting out from a need to prove yourself, if you had started out from an understanding that you can choose your part of the contribution to the world based on what your core liking is, then you would have proceeded to give to the world that which is special with you. You wouldn't have invested your energies in running a business empire that supplies products and services which are not a part of your core liking. If you had proceeded from the right foundational thought, then scaling up wouldn't have been an obsession with you.

If you had started out with the right FT, then you would have enjoyed the daily routines of your work. You would not have been doings things just in order to figure in the first page of the newspapers. Scaling up is a never-ending spiral and anyone who wants to reach the pinnacle, is fooling himself because there is no such thing as a pinnacle to reach when it comes to scaling up in business. As you grow more, the potential for growth increases, too!

N: So, the right FT would be…

P: The right Foundational Thought would to be the one that includes a comprehensive understanding of your life. And not just proceeding from a partial understanding...!

N: What do you mean by comprehensive understanding?

P: To give you one simple example – your grandfather was alive some time ago, he was very much a part of your reality a few years ago, and now he is gone, he has disappeared from this earth. Isn't it?

N: Hey, will you stop this non-sense? What do you know of my grandfather? He is very much alive and he is hardly fifty meters away from us. Can you see him there under that canopy below the neem tree? He is doing some gardening there. How can you say that he is dead when he is very much alive? You seem to lack accuracy!

P: Mr. Naught, I was talking about your paternal grandfather. I know the one who is out there is your maternal grandfather.

For a minute, he was disappointed that the parrot won this time, too. A desire to defeat the parrot was lurking in him! Generally, Mr. Naught wouldn't brook his opponent winning at all. But he gathered himself sufficiently and proceeded.

N: I accept, yes, my paternal grandfather is no more. But why talk about him now?

P: Like him, one day you will also become dead, won't you?

N: (Mr. Naught became furious) What a negative character you are! What an inauspicious creature you are! You are talking about my death when I am sitting here alive, hale and healthy.

P: I only said 'one day' you will become dead, too. I did not say you will die today. Stop being emotional on hearing the word death! Death in your life is as concrete a reality as your breath happening now! Don't you have the maturity to accept the theoretical fact that all of us will die one day?

N: Yes, I accept. I am happy you have included yourself, too! Yes, yes, one day you will die, too!

P: How child-like and childish you are!

N: (with a facial expression of indignance) Yes, I am! Will you please proceed?

P: This thought should be one of the component-thoughts forming your FT.

N: Utter non-sense! Why do you want me to think of my death when I am involved in living my life, running my business? Is there any logical connection?

P: Yes, there is! Although, these two aspects of life-death and running a business seem totally unconnected, in reality they are!

N: How is that possible? Explain to me.

P: See, earlier I said that as is the foundation, so is the building. If you proceed from a need to prove as your FT, then whatever choices you make afterwards in life, go only to reinforce the original FT! So, the moment you choose your FT, consciously or unconsciously, you are sealing the direction of your destiny! One major decision governs one million small decisions.

When you keep a set of healthy thoughts to serve as your FT, you will choose a direction in life which is healthier and balanced. So, healthy foundational thoughts are a must if you want to conduct your life in a wonderful and all-inclusive way. Let us use computer language and let us give a new name to the collection of Foundational Thoughts. Let's call it an FT folder!

N: Ok, I buy your thought. Now, assuming I started afresh today and I was going to choose my Foundational Thoughts, what else would I have to include in my FT folder? I have already included the thought-component that however young today I am, one day my body will age and I will die and be gone!

P: Planet consciousness!

10. Planet Consciousness

N: What do you mean by planet consciousness?

P: That you live on a planet, earth!

N: What nonsense! Any kindergarten child will know this!

P: But is it a part of your FT? Or was it a part of your FT when you started your business life?

N: (a little embarrassed to admit) No. It was not.

P: Then why talk about a child knowing this! I am now talking to you, not to anyone else, or about anyone else!

N: Aren't you rude, Ms. Parrot, for the size you are?

P: Don't go by size. Go by the content!

A thought runs in Mr. Naught's mind this parrot was overly garrulous! But then, he did not want to stop the flow.

N: Now, tell me what has this planet consciousness got to do with my business?

P: You should have this FT that you are living on planet earth with limited geometrical dimensions. Your earth has limited resources, in terms of minerals and crude oil. And what you call your business ambition should not exceed the sustainability threshold of the planet. In other words, whatever you do in business, whatever you do as business should be tempered with sustainability.

N: Why should I care about all this? I am obsessed with my own success in life. What matters to me most is my success!

P: This is proof enough to show that your FT folder needs some alignment. How can you choose to care about your well-being and ignore the well-being of the planet on which you conduct your life of business and business of life?

N: Does everyone think of this?

P: I am talking to you.

N: See, see, again you are becoming rude.

P: I was matter of fact.

Mr. Naught develops a doubt if the parrot was rude or if he was himself intolerant!

N: Okay, I accept my perception was colored. You are not rude. I perceived it that way.

P: The same way your FT is colored and skewed!

N: Simply because I am keeping quiet, you are using strong words against me, Ms. Parrot!

P: I appreciate that humility in you. You are a gentleman.

N: Oh, looks like you want something from me! That is why you are showering praises on me.

P: I don't need any favors. I am living my life as per nature's instruction. I eat from trees and sleep on trees! I live by instinct. But you guys live by a mind. And that makes all the difference!

N: Enough of your philosophy. Now tell me, I have included planet consciousness, included death and what else to include in my FT folder?

P: So, will you stop bribing the pollution-control authorities? Will you properly process the waste discharged from your garment manufacturing units? Will you support the cause of alternative fuels research?

N: Sure, I will…!

P: So, one day you will die and go…

N: (hastily) Don't talk about my death again and again so explicitly! I have told you that I have already included death in my FT folder.

P: Fine. Why touch your sensitive subject! You have included planet consciousness, too! Now, purpose of life.

11. Do you have a purpose, Mr. Naught?

N: What is your thought on purpose of life?

P: The purpose of life is a life of purpose!

N: Yes, I know that. That's what I have been following. I found my purpose to be building a business empire, and hence I have devoted my life time to it!

P: Wait, wait, it is not true that you have found your purpose. Your purpose cannot be running a business. Running a business is the means to an end. You are confused between the means and the end.

N: Will you please clarify it a bit more?

P: The purpose lies buried within you. You should allow that purpose to unfold. But if you allow your borrowed desires to occupy your mind entirely, a lifetime will pass without knowing that purpose. All your life you will mistake your borrowed desires to be your purpose. And when borrowed desires become your FT, you start building your super-structure on that!

N: Now tell me, I had a desire to grow my business. Was that a borrowed desire? I did not consciously borrow it from anyone.

P: Still, it is a borrowed desire!

N: Aren't you losing your wits, Ms. Parrot? I thought you were intelligent!

P: I dare say that your desire to build your business was a borrowed desire! It is because you never allowed your buried purpose to surface at all!

N: Okay, give me a way out. How do I find my purpose?

P: Sit in non-meditation every day for half an hour!

N: If I don't?

P: Nature won't!

N: {puzzled} Nature won't……?

P: Nature won't let you know your purpose!

N: So, doing non-meditation is so important?

P: Yes, certain things come as a result of doing the right things in life!

N: What if I find out, after doing a lot of non-meditation that my purpose is, say for example, to work towards alleviating the suffering of the blind people in the world?

P: Work on that!

N: But without business how can I support that cause?

P: Without knowing that purpose, what significance does your business have?

N: Do you mean to say money-making should be the process that takes me towards fulfilling my purpose?

P: Yes.

N: Is there no meaning to money-making for the sake of money-making?

P: Yes, there is.

N: Don't contradict yourself. What are you trying to say?

P: Money-making in itself is a meaningful process. Money makes your life happen the way you want! Money makes you capable of buying all that you need in life. Money ploughs back into business and hence makes sure the business process continues and it is a never-ending loop. But what is your relation with the business? What is your equation with the business?

N: Understood. I should not be pursuing business for the sake of business. I should be living my life in pursuit of fulfilling my identified purpose. Otherwise, whatever be the scale of business that I reach, I will not feel satisfied at the end of my life. Is that what you are saying?

P: See, the human mind is a pattern-builder. The foundation determines the nature of the pattern. Whatever be the foundation you have, right or wrong, the mind goes on building the superstructure endlessly on that foundation. What if the very foundation is wrong?

N: How can building a business empire ever become wrong?

P: There will never be anything wrong with building a business empire. But the desire to build that empire could itself be wrong!

N: Business, when built, makes money, provides employment, manufactures goods and provides services...! How can business be wrong?

P: Mr. Obsessed, will you listen to me properly? The business process itself need not be wrong. Your desire could be. Yes, if your desire, that foundational desire, is a need to prove yourself, then everything is wrong about you!

N: Why is this need to prove there?

P: it is an expression of your own feelings of inadequacy. It is the default psychological mechanism. The deeper the inadequacy, the greater the need to prove yourself. The outer just reflects the inner.

N: What is wrong in creating an endlessly growing business? Is it not fun?

P: It could be fun to you. But not to mother earth. Mother earth has limited space and limited resources. Mother earth provides enough to fulfil every man's need, but not his greed, said Mahatma Gandhi. As we discussed, it is better that every businessman includes planet consciousness in his FT folder! The very addition of this planet consciousness to the FT folder will trigger new ways of modifying the existing, outdated technologies!

N: Okay, let us move on.

12. Meaning of Life

P: Yes, you have planet consciousness, death, and purpose of life in your FT folder. Now, meaning of life.

N: How different is *purpose of life* from *meaning of life*?

P: Consider this question, `What is the meaning of life?'. There is an error in this question. Can you point it out?

N: No, there seems to be no error in the sentence. It is grammatically perfect.

P: Mr. Naught, not in the grammar! In the meaning part of it!

N: In the meaning? I don't think so.

P: If you look at it, as the author of the famous book, 'Man's Search for Meaning', Dr. Victor Frankl says, every man should think that *it is life* which is asking this question to him or her. You are not supposed to ask *life* for a meaning. Rather, you should know that it is *life* that is asking you, "Hey, Mr. Naught, what is the meaning of *your* life?". So, the general question, 'What is the meaning of life?' is a little limited! What you call 'your life' happens within *a larger field of fixed meaning!*

Generally, in common parlance, we refer to this as *the life process on planet earth.*

N: Does that `life process on earth' stipulate how the lives of individual beings are to roll out?

P: Not when it comes to details. The life process on earth, as concerns human beings, stipulates that every individual human being shall live his life between his birth and death, that he will fulfil a purpose which represents a sort of continuation from his previous births and that during the course of his life he shall work towards liberation from the cycles of birth and death!

N: Why should one work towards the liberation from the cycles of life birth and death?

P: The yogic lore says that unless one works towards liberation, the loop of rebirth and death will continue endlessly. Every single human being invariably seeks a reunion with his own inner nature. But he starts searching in the wrong direction. He identifies himself with the body and the moment this identification is born, he starts searching in the wrong direction. He says his goal is to reach the East but he speeds up in his jet plane towards the West! He goes at break-neck speed towards his goal, but in the opposite direction! The more he travels, the farther he goes away from the goal. Instead of searching his inner nature by turning inward, he starts searching outside through the pleasures and goals of body-mind.

He forgets the fact that it is his inner nature who is the wholesale supplier of all the happiness in the world!

N: A little difficult to grasp! Hope you are not misleading me simply because I have the humility to listen to you!

P: See, even in humility, there is pride!

N: Hush, hush, enough of your supercilious attitude. Now tell me how do I know that I am in search of my own inner nature and not more and more of success? How do I know I am searching for my own inner self through wrong means?

P: That is easy. Monitor your feelings! No amount of material success leaves you a fulfilled and happy man, although you cover it up with your emotional appreciation of your own material successes. Deep inside, you know you have not found what you have been seeking!

N: True.

P: What is true?

N: In my case, it is true.

P: What? You mean to say, in spite of all the successes, you still feel you are missing something?

N: Yes!

P: May be the current level of success is not sufficient for you to be satisfied! You need to achieve more in order to feel fulfilled!

N: Stop joking. I am sensing some kind of mental pain in me. I have come to a stage where the thought of expanding my business any further does not have so much of fizz, nor am I in a position to get out of that swirl.

P: So, you have started asking the big question – 'What is the meaning of *my* life?'

N: In a way yes!

P: Better late than never!

N: Again, you are being sarcastic!

P: I am being matter-of-fact!

N: Enough of your repartee!

P: Now that you have included 'meaning' in your FT folder! Tell me what the real meaning to your life is!

N: I think I want to find union with my inner self directly, instead of trying to indirectly search for myself through material successes. It is proof enough, going by current success levels, that the path of success is unending and it is an ever-growing ladder and one cannot scale it fully because the more one scales, the more the ladder grows, too! Restricting the meaning of my life only to success in material plane does not seem to take me anywhere. I want to break out of this loop! Even If I monopolized all the businesses of the world, I think I would still be missing something!

P: Fantastic. I did not expect this from you so soon!

N: You have said certain things that I cannot ignore. My conscience says you are speaking about an inescapable truth! Self-honesty has started restructuring my personality.

P: So, are you going to say good bye to your businesses and walk out an ascetic tomorrow onwards?

N: Do you suggest that?

P: Yes and no.

N: Don't talk like a confused idiot. Either say yes or no.

P: No and yes.

N: I think you are in a playful mood whereas I am in a sort of angst. My life's road is forking into two. I had been in peace. This afternoon, I don't know from where you came, you have spoilt my peace of mind!

P: Lie!

N: How dare you call me a liar?

P: I said what you said was a lie. You are not a liar.

N: Why do you say it is a lie? I was really in peace before meeting you!

P: You were not in peace; you were in pieces, two pieces!

N: Stop! Stop! You talk too much. I am really losing my cool…

P: You will invite more trouble for yourself by losing your cool! You will spoil your health!

N: Okay, let us not argue. Why did you say I was in two pieces?

P: One part of you was driving you crazy with thoughts about business expansion. Another part was sending feelings of objection!

N: Who is the real me?

P: Neither of them!

N: Do you meant to say I am just nothing and thin air?

P: Not even thin air!

N: Then what am I?

P: Nothing!

N: Are you trying to belittle me?

P: No, raising your status!

N: Don't make yourself an object of mockery. You call me 'nothing' and you say I should think of that as a pride-worthy status!

P: Yes, my yogi friend always says that as we penetrate the depths of our own consciousness, we will experience ourselves as nothing. Did not the Buddha say, 'empty, empty, everything is empty'?

N: Is it all practically possible to know?

P: People who have known this have said this!

N: Where is the proof that they have known?

P: Now, you are using the intellect that you acquired in this life-time and you are using that intellect to know things, isn't it? You tend to hold your intellect as the highest truth within you! Please understand that you are using that intellect but it is not you! Drop that intellect and there you are!

N: Confusing! But smacks of truth! So, your point is that right now I remain *something* and my aspiration is to experience myself as *nothing*.

P: No, your aspiration is to know that you are that nothing!

N: How strange, all these years I thought life was about going from nothing to something. Now you are saying life is about going from something to nothing. But if these thoughts were to be a part of the FT folder of an individual, one would end up doing nothing! One would not entertain any huge desires and without desires humanity cannot make progress at all! I have doubts in your teachings. You are anti-human; you are anti-growth!

P: What is the yard-stick you are using to call me anti-growth?

N: Because you want human beings to become nothing.

P: I am not asking them to become nothing. I do see this with my own eyes that literally every human being is craving to find union with his or her own Self. Is it not obvious to you that everybody is craving madly something or other? They work towards it, attain it only to feel empty again. Is this not true?

N: Yes, this is true. But I am not accepting your statement that everyone in their core is *nothingness*.

P: See, don't forget that we were discussing the meaning of life. The field within which human life operates has pre-fixed laws subject to which human lives can happen! There is no exception! But people vary in their thoughts about this reality. The variation in their thoughts does not alter the reality in any way! Everyone is born with their karmic baggage, everyone continues to live and accumulate further karma, die and be reborn to exhaust some portion of their old karma! Man's ultimate effort should be to get out of this cycle! It is a matter of individual choice! But the ultimate scheme is pre-fixed, whether you accept it or not!

N: So, you say that my life operates within this field too and hence I am also subject to the very same process, isn't it? Now, I am confused. Should I entertain a material desire or should I entertain a spiritual desire? How will I know?

P: Mr. Naught, I am a little tired. Can we continue this discussion some other day?

N: No, no, please don't leave. If you want something to eat, I can give you some biscuits and tea.

P: No thanks, let me eat the fruits here. Ask me your questions.

N: You have confused me. Now, tell me, what should I do in life?

P: Depends on what you want to do.

N: I find meaning in both.

P: Then pursue both.

N: When will I know I am ready to leave all this material drama and go back to unite with my own Self?

P: Non-meditation will unfold the path for you. Don't be impatient.

N: You have unnecessarily modified my ego by making me include all these thoughts in my FT folder.

P: You mean to say you love being egoistic?

N: Yes, that ego, that inadequacy, that need to prove, gave me no time to think. These things always pushed me into endless action in business. Now, you have done damage to me by diluting my ego!

P: Ego stands for a mental state whose underlying emotions are made of negative energy. Feelings of helplessness push themselves forward in the form of a need to prove oneself. This need never gets satisfied because it rests on wrong foundations. On wrong foundations right buildings cannot be constructed. So, you should be happy your ego is diluted with more knowledge about life!

N: You mean to say, one's ego will get diluted if one added more knowledge about life?

P: Yes, that's what happened to you in the last two hours or so!

Just then, both of them hear the heavy blasting sound of fighter jets flying past overhead.

13. Ego Modification

N: Now that you have modified my ego! Do you think it is possible to modify the egos of those people who order these warplanes around? Political leaders seem to have a rock-solid ego than what we have.

P: Political leaders are of two kinds. One kind of politicians is motivated to continue in politics because of their deep-rooted insecure feelings that they experienced early in life. Remember, everyone always carries his past with him! So, they try to compensate their hollow feelings with political power. The limited, temporally limited power to get a few things done according to their commands, gives them the feeling that they are invincible. But, in nature's eyes, they are the same – a pauper is as good as the President!

The second kind of politicians is good-natured. They operate from an original Foundational Thought. They know that their passion towards governance will help humanity live a more organized, more progressive and systematic kind of life. And hence they continue to offer their services. Power and pelf will not motivate them. But they take pride in their self-assessment that they are *good politicians*!

N: In any case, people have to have some ego, isn't it? Either they must alter their Foundational Thoughts to include life's truths or they must be motivated by some raw inadequate feelings about themselves! So, every human being can be found to belong to either one of these camps. Don't you think so?

P: You are right.

N: Now tell me, which kind of politicians is responsible for the continuation of wars and preparation for wars.

P: The self-aware ones!

N: Sounds preposterous. How is it possible? As per your thinking, only those people who proceed from inadequacy and insecurity will have egos that will pave way for confrontation. How do you say that the self-aware category is responsible for continuation of wars?

P: Knowing is not doing.

N: What do you mean by that?

P: The self-aware category knows that it is futile for humanity to spend billions of dollars in construction and purchase of war weapons. But they have not done anything to put an end to this trend. To that extent, they are responsible for the continuation of war orientation.

N: I am not convinced.

P: Now, tell me, which of the two categories really has the capability, in case they wished, to change the trend of wars and preparation for wars? The first category is helplessly glued to the possibility of war and aggression and they cannot think beyond it. The second category knows that wars may be a possibility or may not be a possibility!

N: I think it is the second category that can do something in this direction of eliminating wars and preparation for wars!

P: You are right. But failing to do what needs to be done is as detrimental as doing what should not be done.

N: Are you trying to play a moral authority on mankind?

P: Natural authority!

N: You mean to say nature has authority over mankind's thinking?

P: Yes, you human beings are puppets in the hands of nature's powerful laws!

N: Don't belittle humanity. Did we construct these skyscrapers or did you creatures do it? Did we create these supersonic jets or did you do? Did we create all these space journeys or did you do it? Did we create cell phones and computers or did you guys do?

P: You are defensive.

N: (Mr. Naught feels a little uptight and frazzled) Why then belittle humanity?

P: I was matter of fact. You are all puppets in the hands of nature. Defy nature's ways if you can. Look at your body, now it is 45 years old. A day will come when you are 90 or 100, your skin will wither like a dried leaf. A day will come when the body will give up and you will get separated from your body. Can you stop this from happening?

N: No, I can't. I remember what a handsome and healthy man my paternal grandfather was. But then, a day came when he grew too old and died!

P: So, the manner in which anyone conducts his life will change the moment he realizes the fact that all this is a temporary drama. During the drama, every scene matters. But it is a definite fact that the drama will come to an end one day.

N: Does that stop one from playing his role?

P: No, it only goes to modify the kind of role one plays. In India, there is a practice of people smearing some holy ash/powder on their forehead when they go to temples as well as in the prayer rooms of their house. I am told that this practice is an exercise in bringing life's truth to one's awareness. Whenever people take the ash in their hands and smear it on their forehead, it serves as a reminder that one day their body will be reduced to ashes, too!

N: Quite scary. The thought that one day I will also die dampens me!

P: Why?

N: Why play this drama when it is all going to come to an end!

P: You are right and you are wrong.

N: Again, you have started your non-sense!

P: Sense!

N: How does that make sense? You have made me realize that I am just an actor in the drama called life and that the drama will go on endlessly but my role will come to an end. So, I feel like giving up.

P: This shows you have not found your purpose yet in life. If you have found your over-whelming purpose, you will have the maturity to continue with your work, in spite of knowing fully well that one day your role will come to an end.

N: I am unable to grasp.

P: Now, look at the time that preceded my meeting with you and the time after my meeting. Before meeting me, you were neck-deep involved in business expansion plans. After speaking to me, you have realized that you are constructing a building on a foundation that was not of your choice. At best, it was an unconscious choice. Now, the old motivation is refusing to drive you and your awareness has expanded! Now you know you are living on a planet where resources are limited and that your business desires cannot exceed the threshold of endurance on the part of mother earth; now you know that you have an intrinsic purpose in life; now you know that nature has clearly defined the possibilities for human beings and that you are only an actor playing a role for a temporary period of time!

This knowledge should encourage you rather than discourage you. If you really value yourself, in spite of the fact you are in a sojourn, you should identify a mammoth task that resonates with your core and work towards fulfilling that. You must be able identify some area in human life where you find a lacuna and you should work towards fulfilling it. You should work towards fulfilling your highest ideals that are in keeping with the ideal of the well-being of all. If you are not getting encouraged, it is because you have looked at life as a place from where you wanted to gain something for yourself. You have never looked at life as an opportunity to give something of yourself to the others around!

P: You are talking too much. Don't talk without knowing the facts. Do you know the amount of money that I have spent on corporate social responsibility? Do you know the amount of money I have donated towards AIDs control and rehabilitation of AIDs patients? Do you know how much money I have spent on the poverty-stricken children of the world?

P: You have dealt with the effects, not with the causes!

N: Don't you appreciate the amount of money that I have contributed towards various social welfare schemes?

P: Definitely I appreciate! But diverting that kind of funds towards educating people will make more sense. Educating people on how and why AIDs is happening is more important than alleviating the pains of people who are suffering from AIDs. Educating the starving people to take charge of their lives is more important than giving food to them. Fostering independence is more important than direct feeding. Problems should be addressed at the root level. Treating the symptom will not cure the disease.

N: Do you think it is the job of corporate business houses to take up this kind of educational campaign?

P: Anyway, you guys are already doing it! You guys are involved in funding one rehabilitation scheme or the other. Why not also take up organized educational campaigns? When I say education, I am not talking about skill training – how to write a software program for a bank or how to fly a plane. I am talking about educating people on the basics of life – that it is people's responsibility to take complete charge of their lives, that their life, their well-being is their business and not anybody else's! Rather than showing sympathy towards a starving population, you guys should open their eyes to the truths of life. You guys should motivate them to fend for themselves. It might take a long time. But that is the only solution. For how many days will you go on giving fish to a starving man? You have to teach them to fish. Or give them the idea that if they want to eat properly, they have to find a way to fetch food, too!

N: Makes sense. But, don't you think it is the business of the governments to undertake this kind of campaigns?

P: It is a matter of choice. Fixing the responsibility on the governments is a decent way of escaping. It is basic dishonesty. You want to show that you are doing service to society in the name of corporate social responsibility, but you will only be doing what comes easy. Any amount of money siphoned off towards symptom level social service is never going to bring about long-term well-being for the people concerned.

N: Why do you insist on solving problems at the root level? Does not today's food matter to a starving man?

P: See, we are living in a *cause-and-effect* world. When a cause is removed, the effect will also be removed. Look at the abject poverty prevailing in one of the proverbial parts of the world. The society that we are talking about has chosen to give birth to children unmindful of whether they can feed the children or not. Somehow, the process of childbirth seems to be happening by an unconscious, default tendency. Now, assuming this trend continues, what is the point in you going on giving food to the starving? The ideal logic is that the society concerned should limit the number of children if they don't have the capacity to feed them.

Their first focus, as a society, should be to empower themselves on a war footing so that they can reach a reasonably good level of economic success where their children don't have to die for want of the very first necessity of life, food. When their own survival is in question, why create more children and make them meet miserable conditions? Today's food matters to a starving man. It is divine to give food to a starving man rather than allowing him to die helplessly. But for how many more days and for how many more people and for how long? Don't you think teaching them to take charge of their lives is more a meaningful help?

N: Hmmm….! So, do you mean to say any society is responsible for its own well-being and it should not depend on other countries or societies for anything?

P: In a spirit of give and take, borrowing is fine. Taking a little bit of help is fine. But if a society always looks to the outside world for solutions to its problems, then the society is to blame. Economic independence is the first condition to well-being in a society. Territorial wars and feudal wars of power should not take precedence. Food for everyone should be the natural order. The rulers as well as the ruled should not forget this.

N: Why is that those societies do not realize this?

P: See, in the nature of things, people get stuck with their current problems and their day-to-day problems. When they are stuck in their day-to-day problems, they cannot think of establishing their long-term priorities! Unless an external force intervenes and educates them, they will continue to remain confused. Unless acted upon, human psychological states do not change easily. That's why I am insisting that the big business houses also undertake regular educational and motivational campaigns.

For example, they can undertake a project like this – 'Starvation-free Africa'. Here, the campaign will all be about educating them on the need to take complete charge of their lives rather than giving tons of food. I am not saying they should be allowed to starve. Food can be given, clothes can be given wherever there is need, but these things should be given as the second offering. The first offering should be an eye-opening educational and empowerment campaign. Or at least, both should go hand in hand.

N: Convincing. This idea of dealing with the root of the problem is quite interesting. Recently I have been to some countries in the Southern hemisphere and visited some major countries there. There is growth on all fronts. There spiritual knowledge is at its peak. Education is spreading far and wide and millions of people are graduating every year in computer science and other science subjects. Still, compared to Western standards, some countries seem to be lagging behind in many ways. Do you really know why it is so?

14. Path to Becoming a Super-Power

P: Oh! Countries in Southern hemisphere! It is a beautiful world. As you said, there are spiritually advanced countries. Spirituality is built into the warps and wefts of their everyday life! For example, in villages, they don't sit on a dining table and eat. They sit on the floor with their spine erect. And science says that, during the course of human evolution, it is the spine's erect position which paved way for a speedy development of the brain! They all go to places of worship regularly. There is a saying in India that 'you should not dwell in a village that does not have a temple'. Temples are energy centres. They are like batteries. They charge you free of cost! People have understood this practical help that temples offer and hence they visit churches, mosques and temples at least once in a week. This way I can give your more and more examples. Coming to your question as to why some countries are lagging behind when compared to the Western physical standards, the answer is simple – most, if not all, most of the people there don't practice self-honesty!

N: Strange! Absurd answer! What has self-honesty to do with their lagging behind?

P: Everything! There is a flaw in the FTs most of them carry!

N: What is that flaw in their Foundational Thought process?

P: Lack of self-honesty is that flaw! And this flawed thinking leads to flawed action and the flawed action leads to flawed results! And a never-ending pattern of events gets built on this flawed foundation!

N: Sounds mysterious! Will you explain this further?

P: I will. Just take the example of laying roads in rural areas in some of those countries. The local governments usually award the contract to build roads to companies based on a system of tenders. Different companies submit their tenders and the government opts for the lowest bidder. From the government's point of view, it is fairly justified in that they do not want to spend the public money lavishly. But the companies, out of desperation to get the contract, get into a competitive mode and quote the least possible amount to obtain the contract. Simply because the company quoted the least amount to get the contract, the company, once the contract is obtained, cuts corners on the quality of raw materials and finally it shows up in the poor quality of roads. Here the poor quality is the symptom. And the flaw lies in the root. The flaw lies in the very selection process. Lowest bidding cannot always ensure you get the most qualitative work too. This is known even to the officers of the government.

Still, they continue to practice the same method. See, once the foundation is wrong, the building also turns out to be faulty.

N: Can you give me one more example?

P: When a real estate company obtains a contract to construct a cluster of flats, if it cuts corners, it will show up in the poor quality of the building. Cracks develop on the walls and sometimes even the roof collapses! There have been instances!

And look at bribery. In some countries, bribe has become the norm, from top to bottom!

I have just given simple examples. And everyone knows of many such stories.

N: Why do people commit such mistakes in spite of knowing that it is not good to commit such mistakes? Why do they flout the voice of their conscience?

P: Deep rooted insecurity. Avarice! And keeping up with Joneses!

N: How does insecurity play a role in this?

Life, once born into a body, gets mingled with the body – this the spiritual outlook. Even if you do not believe in a `life' being born inside a human body, you will readily accept that human beings have a physical body, won't you? The physical body is vulnerable to attack and fears dangers. Insecure feeling is present in you right from your birth. So, you humans start seeking security in whatever form it is available. When young, you stick to your parents or whoever is around you for security. When you grow up, you seek security in the form of material possessions – one house, or even more houses, more business so that you can have more money, a dedicated spouse, more security guards to your house, more safety lockers, more fixed deposits in Swiss banks, huge tracts of real estate…see the list is endless. All this instinct to possess things is the result of insecurity. Fulfilling the basic needs is acceptable.

N: Since every human being has a physical body, can they really over-come this insecure feeling? Is it not natural to accumulate more and more so that we can be more secure?

P: More accumulation only will only increase the insecure feelings further. First, it all started as an effort to fulfil one's needs. When you accumulate more than your need, protecting that wealth and business becomes an even bigger responsibility. For so many reasons of image, ego and deeper insecure feelings, you become a prisoner to these things.

N: What is the way out?

See, material objects and possessions are a must if want to live a lifetime on earth. Here you should look at the question of how much of is needed! Survival is a question of fulfilling three basic needs – food, clothes and shelter. Ensuring this is basic survival process. Once this is taken care of, you proceed to acquire the luxuries of life. If you acquire some luxuries out of a sense of aesthetics or with an intention to enjoy the utility of those things, it is different. But, when fear drives you to acquire wealth endlessly, you become a prisoner and not a master of your own psychological process. This is what is very important to understand. Today, a little work ensures the survival for everyone. We are not living in a jungle where might is right. We have become a civilization and we have invented the most precious thing that could ever happen on earth!

N: What is that most precious thing?

P: Government!

N: You mean politicians?

P: Go deeper, Mr. Naught. Don't be naive. I meant the concept of governance and not the actual governments of countries. Today, human society is hugely different from animal world in that you have invented government – a small number of people elected by all the people and the small number is invested with all the powers to run a setup which will take care of the well-being of all! So, in today's world, with the diverse kind of services and products on offer, no one has to feel insecure. Everyone is a part of the system and in that system everybody else contributes towards your own well-being. You don't have to cultivate your own crop, you don't have to clean your drainage, you don't have to stitch your own shirt, you don't have to run police set up, you don't have to manufacture your automobile, you don't have to sit as a judge in the court, you don't have to construct your own house, but everything is made available to you because of others' contribution. You just have to contribute your part, whatever it is.

N: So...

P: So, you have to start living life from a perspective of truth, and not a perspective of insecurity.

N: How does keeping up with Joneses play a role in making people violate their own inner voice?

P: This is the worst psychological disease mankind can ever have! People forget the fact that their needs are entirely different from those of others. You might love having a beautiful wife, another might believe in having an average-looking wife but a beautiful house! Simply because the other person owns a beautiful house, you should also not jump into it. Your neighbor might own a private jet with a built-in swimming pool. But your desire might be to swim in a nice resort amidst a natural setting. Simply because your neighbor does it, you should also not do it. Here, people do not understand this. They get carried away. A life time is devoted to keeping up with Joneses. Nature has not produced photo-copies of human beings. It has made every single individual unique and un-replicable!

N: How do we correct the situation?

P: Acceptance. One should accept the truth about one's own life. For example, if a government employee who has chosen to receive fixed monthly emoluments chooses to compete with his neighbor who is a businessman, will it do good to him? If he does, he will become debt-ridden. Catching up with others will only bring trouble to oneself. You being who are is much more important and in that lies a successful and peaceful life. If those self-dishonest societies understand these two points, their creativity and trustworthiness credentials will go up tremendously!

N: Tell me this, are the political leaders of those countries also like this? Aren't they different?

P: No, the entire social hierarchy lacks self-honesty in their day-to-day life. There, assume a person wants to start a business and applies for some license from the government. He opts for the bribery route to obtain that license in spite of not meeting all the requirements! Giving bribe to get things done is a way of life in many countries. People have no qualms about giving bribe because they don't want their projects to be delayed. The officials have their conscience pricking but then they get carried away by comparing themselves with the rich people in society. A government job pays fixed salaries and there is no room for earning much extra income, however sincere they are. People know this very well at the time of opting for a government job. It was after all their own choice to settle for a fixed salary job.

At the time of choosing this job, this job was a great boon for them. Once they get settled, and once they spend a decade or two in their jobs, they realize that they are stuck with the job and there is no alternative way to earn more money. Seeing other people spend money lavishly, these people also get carried away and they somehow want to make quick bucks and they start insisting on bribes. In several countries, from a municipal officer to a minister in the Central cabinet, they don't hesitate to take bribe to discharge their obligatory duties. Bribe is a way of life, so to say!

N: How is this bribery affecting the growth of the country? Anyway, people are getting things done and growth is happening, right?

P: No, bribery eats into the very quality of the nation. In the case of the government officials taking bribe, it is a clear case of people practicing self-dishonesty. See, take again the case of an official in a government job. First of all, it is he who, in full awareness, valued this government job and chose to settle in the job for fixed monthly salaries. But then, if in the middle he realizes he wants to have a different life-style, he should have the courage to resign the job and start a business or seek a private employment. That is the right, logical thinking. Trying to satisfy his extra wants through the bribery route leads to compunction and the person suffers internally although he buys the luxuries for himself. Such violation of self-honesty not only lowers the quality of the individual, but also the quality of the social fabric of which he is a part.

N: Do you mean to say that bribe paves way for ignoring of the quality of products and services?

P: Absolutely, yes. When an official who is in charge of issuing driving license takes bribe and issues a license to an untrained person, he becomes responsible for the death of, may be, some qualitative people in the country, too! In an accident, the untrained driver might end up killing, unwittingly, a consequential person! The reckless driver might end up killing an important and knowledgeable person in society. Who knows? Now go to the roots. Why should an official issue license to a person without inspecting his skill levels? Isn't the officer getting paid for doing this specific task? See, one error might create a chain of errors!

Use of cheap construction materials has many times ended up in the collapse of buildings! Adulteration in packaged food items spoils the health of the general public. When bribery enters the area of defence purchases, precious lives could be lost due to faulty engineering!

N: So, when we compromise on quality, we set in motion a chain reaction of bad results. Is that what you are saying?

P: Yes, I am sure you have heard of the story, ` For want of a shoe, the horse was lost. For want of a horse, the rider was lost. For want of a rider, the battle was lost. For want of a battle, the kingdom was lost. And all for the want of a horseshoe nail.' The same way, because of lack of self-honesty on the part of individuals, the nation becomes the victim, finally!

N: Now, will the politicians ever become self-honest?

P: Politicians may not become self-honest, but self-honest people can enter politics!

N: That sounds good. Earlier you suggested that business houses should also undertake to educate people of the world in the basics. Supposing I were to take up a campaign to educate the people of the world, what messages would I give?

P: Every citizen should live in honesty to his own self. What he knows to be his truth, he should live that truth. If someone decides to take up a government job, let him stick to it in all self-honesty and lead a life within the salaries. He can, in fact, prepare his children for a life of business or high-salary jobs!

At the political level, the politicians should also know that the political offices are not business houses for them to earn money. Politics is for serving people and business is for making money. Simple honesty! Right now, there is flaw in their thinking. They think that Politics is for making money. They want to sail the airplane on the ocean and fly the ship in the skies! See, there are always the fringe benefits – like power, respect and wealthy atmosphere for them to enjoy. But, when money-making becomes the aim, they should switch to business or high-paying job.

N: And what about the common man? How is an average citizen to practice self-honesty?

15. National Well-Being Through Individual Self-Honesty

P: There is a saying, `your character is what you are in the dark'. Self-acceptance and self-respect lead to practicing of self-honesty and vice versa. If one knows what one's preferences are, then he should stick to them under all circumstances. Supposing a guy believes in living his life driving a small car, he should not get carried away when he sees someone driving a swanky one. If driving a swanky one is his original choice, then he can work towards buying one. The point here is that he should not get carried away when he sees his colleagues buy costlier stuff.

Comparing oneself with others distorts one's thinking, makes one self-dishonest. Honesty to one's self means honesty to one's own preferences and choices, too. One cannot live one's life always in comparison with others. If one wants to ape others, then one will forget one's own identity. Every human being is unique in his choices and everyone should respect his own or her own identity. There is beauty in this acceptance of oneself. I am not saying people should settle for mediocre things. No. But each one should accept one's own desires for what they are! Simple honesty!

N: Now I feel like talking to you with some respect, Ms. Parrot. You have some genuine concern for the people of the world. Now, tell me what is the relationship between self-honesty and integrity levels in a society?

P: See, there is no such thing as integrity. There is only self-honesty. What is inside is what is outside. When people are self-dishonest, they cannot show integrity to others in their dealings. What comes first is self-honesty. If a person practices honesty with himself, he will automatically practice honesty with others. When a person respects his own truth, he will respect the truth with others, too.

N: Why does this self-dishonesty happen?

P: Primarily because of one's insecure feelings. Survival needs make a person self-dishonest. Secondly because of a lack of knowledge and thinking! They just start aping others. The lure of the luxuries of life makes some people derail.

N: Is there anything wrong with the luxuries of life?

P: No, there is nothing wrong about possessing and enjoying the luxuries of life. But one has to work towards it. Trying to obtain something without working for it is not the right thing. If someone buys a television set with the money that he got as bribe, every time he sees the TV, he will experience a mild pricking deep inside him. And he can never escape this pricking even on his death bed. Because, his conscience, which resides deep inside, knows that he violated the dictates of his own self. I have just given a simple example. And you know of many such stories where people have committed serious violations like embezzlement, connivance of crimes, etc.

N: Now, how to solve this problem of government officials and politicians taking bribes? Can't the government levy more taxes and pay the government officials on par with the private employment? Aren't they sacrificing their lifetime in the service of the people?

P: Yes, it is a possibility. But, even after the hike, people might get tempted to take bribes.

N: So, what do you think is the solution?

P: The only solution is every citizen must be encouraged to practice self-honesty. Over a period of time if everyone starts practicing honesty inside them, it will start showing up on the outside. Practicing self-honesty is a chain reaction kind of a process. People will start believing in simple straight forwardness in all dealings. For example, if an official demands bribe, the citizen might simply say, 'if you want more money, please resign and start a business!' Or when the citizen is offering a bribe, the official will say, 'if you are convinced that everything is proper with you, why do you want to bribe me to pass the file?'

N: So, what you are saying is that people should learn to take the appropriate routes. If they want more money, they should either start a business or join a private enterprise. You acknowledge their right to desiring a wealthy lifestyle but you are saying they should not try to obtain that wealth through the wrong route!

P: Yes, see, today's world is an open world, a world full of opportunities. There is no stopping anyone from becoming wealthy. Anyone can become anything if he wishes to. One can choose one's level of wealth. But one should not end up being a square peg in a round hole.

N: I am still unable to see how the practice of self-honesty can lead to loss of credibility?

P: See, during the 60s, 70s and 80s, there was a craze in some developing countries about anything foreign-made – a tape recorder, or a TV or a watch or a car. Not that these things were not being made in their own countries. But still people preferred foreign made things because they saw the quality in them. In comparison, they understood that foreign-made products were more qualitative. Why were foreign-made products more qualitative and not the ones made at home? One reason is the level of technological knowledge. But the primary reason was the lack of honesty in carrying out the production processes. At every stage, there was compromise. You don't have to do an elaborate investigation to find out if compromise has been made on the raw materials and production process because the quality just reflects in the end product.

If you make a car engine which breaks down every 1000 kms, then there must be a great compromise on the quality. If you make a watch which stops working within 6 months, then it shows the compromise. If you make a computer whose hard disk collapses within 6 months, then there is compromise! A car engine could run either half a million kms or just 50,000 kms – it depends on the quality of raw materials and process!

N: So, do you mean to say that people in the developed countries practice more self-honesty and that is why they respect the quality of their products and intuitively respect their customers, too?

P: Yes, no amount of external regulation will make these self-dishonest countries on par with developed societies unless they correct themselves at the root level and not at the symptom level. One thousand laws cannot make a person a reliable one as the practice of self-honesty can! The need of the hour is not external laws but the need of the hour is internal laws.

N: Why are you using the plural form – internal laws? Do you have anything in addition to self-honesty?

P: Yes, I have one more potent internal law. It is an appreciation of cause and effect.

16. To Create an Effect, Create the Cause

N: What does this mean? How can an appreciation of cause and effect help these countries become a super power?

P: This law will help not only these Southern countries, but any nation on earth to become a superpower.

N: And will you throw more light?

P: Yes, see, the human minds are awareness machines. And the mind tends to be in awareness of a huge collection of memories – knowledge files, belief files, information files, etc. Unless we accentuate a particular file, the file does not find prominence and execution.

N: I am not getting it.

P: See, what you focus on grows. What you focus on finds practical manifestation. In this light, these developing societies should make a deliberate focus on the law of cause of effect.

N: Is it a constitutional law?

P: Don't act too innocent. It is a natural law.

N: What is the connection between cause of effect and a country becoming a super-power?

P: I will explain. See we live in a world where the law of cause of effect rules. Causes create effects. Efforts produce results. The quantity of cause is the quantity of effect. The quantity of effort is the quantity of result. By the same token, the quantity and quality of the output is directly proportional to the quantity and quality of the input!

Assuming we created a `hard work and efforts' ladder of 0 to 100 and arranged all countries on a hierarchy, whoever is at the top is there by virtue of the quality and quantity of causes they have created over a period of time! They did not attain that status overnight. Beneath their success lies decades of hard work! And if a country in the Southern hemisphere wants to reach the 100th rung, then it should calculate the quantity of causes needed in order to reach that position. And then, it should start taking the route of implementation of those qualitative causes in a systematic manner. And this should happen in all areas of life – from agriculture to aviation to IT to services and so on.

N: What will this *massive cause and effect* route mean to an individual in his day-to-day life?

P: This will mean that every citizen of these countries, whichever field he works in, will start quantifying his own cause and effect. He will first fill the gap in his own life. Supposing an executive in a software company realizes that he can put in 50% more work per month when compared to the current level, then, he should make efforts, of his own accord, to live up to his 100% potential. When everyone does this, within a decade, their productivity will increase manifold. There will be a gradual progress not only in the quantity of the services and products, but also in the quality of the products and services. When the quality of products and services goes up, a huge credibility record will get built. Quality will speak for itself and it will start attracting quantity.

N: How can we open the eyes of people to this law of cause and effect?

P: It is simple. You should run a campaign to this effect that every individual is the architect of his own destiny. Where he stands today is the direct result of the causes that he has either produced or failed to produce! Mr. Naught, understand that no individual on earth will work enthusiastically for the sake of others! One will only work for oneself!

If you say someone has dedicated his life for the sake of others' well-being, the truth is he has not! He could have donated huge monies for noble causes. But he has not done it for others. Basically, he has done it for himself, he has only fulfilled a need felt within himself. He has only helped himself! He has just fulfilled his desideratum! Without feeling that need, how can he choose to help others? The psychological process begins and ends with a person. The impact on others is just a by-product. But, such a desire to help others is the trademark of evolved beings!

So, you should motivate every individual to measure his own success levels in the light of this law of cause and effect. See, entropy or lethargy can cause deep downward spirals in human progress. Unless men and women are taught to rise against the downward pull, they will remain a victim to this second law of thermodynamics.

N: What does this second law of thermodynamics say?

P: It says the natural tendency of material objects is to fall towards chaos and disintegration! And human beings have a material body! Now, you will get an idea of the importance of the spirit when you equate the word 'spirit' to the word 'self' in self-honesty. So, when we say you are self-honest, it is as good as saying you are spirit-honest! You are honest to the spirit, or the self. And the spirit and the self are not material in nature! So, if you want to fight the material body's tendency towards disorganization and chaos, you should take the help of the 'self' which is spirit. And hence the importance of self-honesty!

N: Oh, that's a wonderful way of understanding the fight between the body and the spirit. I understand that unless we take the help of the invisible spirit, we cannot change the visible!

P: So, the practice of self-honesty has much deeper implications! It will make a nation get grounded in spirit!

N: Do you think that these two laws are enough for any country to emerge a superpower?

P: Yes, the practice matters. It is the duty of every individual to practice these values as what he practices at his individual level has a way of affecting the whole scenario. The part will affect the whole and whole will affect the part. Everyone can contribute towards the clean and strong image of a nation by sticking to these values. When the country itself carries the reliability tag, everyone can benefit from it. So, what they get is simply the result of what they give!

N: In a way, what you are saying is that 'altruism is nothing but the height of self-honest selfishness'.

P: Yes, you are right. If one really wants to take care of his own self, he should take care of the whole. Supposing you want an uninterrupted and steady supply of drinking water to your house, you should work towards the goal of everyone in the city getting drinking water in an uninterrupted manner. You should not be working on ingenious ways to get the supply only to *your* house. When others don't have it, they will snatch it from you.

N: I have understood. Now, tell me from your own understanding of how the human mind works, is there an easy way to program these values in the minds of people?

P: Yes, simple. Raise slogans to the specific effect you want to create. For example, look at this slogan that can be raised by a nation, 'Our people are self-honest'. And display this everywhere through physical posters, electronic messages and oral reinforcements in school/ college prayers.

N: Sounds too simplistic!

P: Our greatest truths are the simplest! If you are used to expecting complicated answers then you should ask someone else who has done a Ph.D. on life!

N: Don't get angry. A mature parrot like you getting angry is not understandable.

P: Contradiction in terms!

N: what do you mean?

P: A parrot and maturity!

N: But you are!

P: You are not!

N: Don't tease me like this. In a way, my ego has melted, and I have started looking up to you with respect for your valuable insights!

P: I have to go home!

N: It is hardly 5.45 pm. You can fly home even at 7 p.m. as this is summer and there is so much of sun light.

P: You are wasting my time.

N: Ok, I am sorry. Now, you said creating the right slogans and spreading them will help create the reality corresponding to the slogan, isn't it?

P: Yes.

N: But tell me this, just saying and spreading the slogans – will it create the reality corresponding to the slogans?

P: Yes, but a lot depends on the content of the slogans. And practice! If the slogans, in themselves, do not have an uplifting effect on people, they will fail. But people will slowly start accepting that which is beneficial to themselves and society.

N: What other slogans can, say, India display?

P: 'Our country loves cause and effect', 'Our country respects itself' and 'Our country is reliable', 'Our country loves quality', `Our country is a pioneer' and so on. One day, all these slogans will become the collective consciousness of the people of the country. See, seeds have a way of sprouting at the right time.

N: How often should every citizen hear this or see this message?

P: As often as possible in a day.

N: Will this really help every citizen of these countries? Some could argue that practice of self-honesty will deprive them of an opportunity to live their life happily because they can no longer accept bribes! And they might choose to flout self-honesty because it prevents extra income!

P: If they are unduly happy today, they will be miserable tomorrow. If they are in restraint today, they will be in bliss tomorrow. Because, people will always carry their past with them! And the past will not spare them!

N: Are you talking about any poetic justice? Is there an all-knowing God with an excel sheet to shell out punishment if people violated self-honesty?

P: No, that God is not external. He resides within each person. He will turn himself into barbs and needles when a person violates the tenets of healthy living.

N: Who cares?

P: Don't you care?

N: I....do care! But then...

P: You have done enough of bribing people and I know that your business empire was built partly by bribing people in order to clinch deals.

N: Don't say that again! ...Yes, I have bribed people to get things done. But my business empire is the result of my cause and effect.

P: How does that matter? When you flout norms, you can buy the whole world. There is an Oriental saying which goes to this effect, 'a person who does not care for morals, will become even bigger than the King himself.' Success has to be 100% success. Impure success is failure. If not 100%, you should be 99% honest. Do you think, Mr. Naught, you are 99% self-honest?

N: No, I am sorry. I score only 35% on self-honesty in self-assessment.

P: So, material success or business success can happen even without self-honesty! You might wonder why then worry about being self-honest or practice integrity with others!

N: Yes, why bother about self-honesty or integrity!

P: When we find someone behaving in a contemptuous manner, we call him a 'pig'. We don't call him a sparrow or a lion or a deer! Pigs, it is said, don't respect the dignity of even consanguineal relationships when it comes to having sex. Man has an innate sense of what is right and what is wrong, what is desirable and what is not desirable. Mind my word, 'man'. If you are a man or woman, you need to respect your own inner voice which is connected to the beauty and rhythm of this well-ordered, harmonious universe. It is a matter of choice!

N: Do you mean to say human beings should be punished if they don't practice higher values of integrity?

P: No, punishment can only be a deterrent. It can never change a person from being negative to positive.

N: So, what is your conclusion?

P: It is for you to think about!

N: I have come to my own conclusions!

P: Human being or a lesser being?

N: Obviously, human being! I am going to put an end to all devious ways of obtaining and boosting business.

P: The switch will test your endurance.

N: Whatever be the test, I am going to build a new 'organizational culture'.

P: Of what?

N: An organizational culture which has its own healthy Foundational Thoughts!

P: Will bribing be one of the key principles of success?

N: Stop joking, Ms. Parrot. I am seriously changing. I now understand that the honest path is the longest but most enjoyable and a sure passport to success. And I don't have to live in worry about the FBI or CBI chasing me. I will hold my head high and walk with pride.

P: Not so easy.

N: Why are you discouraging me?

P: You will pay a price if reversed your practices overnight.

N: So, do you want me to continue the old path?

P: No. Whomever you appreciated for their closure of business deals in spite of their following a hook or crook method, will now become disenchanted with you if you changed your stand now!

N: But I will convince them. In a way, I am responsible for this work culture. As is the father, so is the family! I always encouraged people who would just do it! I never bothered about the means. All that mattered to me was the end result.

P: Means have to justify the end, too, said Mahatma Gandhi.

N: I understand. People do live their lives with a gap in their understanding of the life process! I have been one among them! I have lived life with partial understanding! Now, I admit I have flouted norms but have decided never to do it again.

P: Why?

N: I am changed.

P: How?

N: Your words.

P: Can words change people as easily?

N: The truth behind your words.

P: Can I trust your change?

N: If you have any doubt, come to my New York office next year this time around. I will show you the list of changes.

P: Can I take leave?

N: It is hardly 6.00 p.m. Why don't you stay back for some more time?

P: You can ask me the last few questions. Do you have any?

N: Yes, what is it that you are getting in return by educating me on the basics of life?

P: Nothing.

N: Why will you waste your time and energy without a reward?

P: There is no basis in reality for your equation.

N: But I believe that every one hour of my time is equal to a few thousand dollars.

P: That is for people scripted in receiving mode.

N: What is this receiving mode? Then, there should be something like a giving mode too, is there such a thing?

P: Yes, people in general practice only receiving. They never think about giving.

N: Yes, I have seen it in my own organizations. The executives, from top to bottom, just want to receive, of course with some exceptions. Their stand is always, 'What is there for me in it?'

P: There is nothing wrong in it.

N: But it was not right, either, I thought.

P: You are right.

N: Should people be taught to give first?

P: Yes, only a few people understand the secret of how the reality works when it comes to receiving.

N: what is that secret?

P: If you want to receive, you should first give!

N: Can I tell my employees to give their dedication first?

P: You can.

N: Will they not ask me to give a handsome salary first?

P: Although you need to practice giving handsome salaries first before taking results from them, the onus is on them to give their dedication first before thinking of receiving handsome salaries.

N: Chicken first or egg first?

P: As an employer, you have a slight degree of upper hand. Human beings are stratified in terms of their age, skill levels and maturity. It is for the employee to accept his station in life and start practicing `giving'. In the long run, he will receive more by virtue of having given more.

N: What do you mean by the employee accepting his station? Is it not demeaning to him?

P: No, only fools will refuse to exercise a sense of realism. A person, however potential he is, has to work through years in order to reach a certain higher level. If you promote an executive suddenly to the level of a General Manager, he cannot withstand there. The necessary skills sets and maturity will be missing. And when one comes to possess the necessary skill sets and maturity, the world will come to know of it automatically.

N: You mean to say a skilled person does not need an advertisement. His actions will speak for themselves?

P: Yes, out of a sense of competition, if one wants to get promoted without possessing the necessary maturity, it will only harm him by making him live on edge all the time. The promotion will prove to be premature. He will be experiencing anxiety all the time. And he might end up goofing up things!

N: So, what you are saying is that the natural order of progress is better!

P: Yes.

N: But why is this urge on the part of my employees to grow faster?

P: Comparison. Greed. All around he sees people with more salaries, a better car and a better house! Does he at the same time see the people who have a smaller house, a smaller car and a smaller salary, etc?

N: So, they should be taught that they will receive in proportion to what they give. And they need not bother about receiving as it is determined by what they give!

P: Yes, it needs some amount of maturity to stick to the giving mode. When you realize that what is in your hands is only giving, you will realize the futility of thinking about receiving.

N: So, I will encourage my teams to think of giving their best, first.

P: Yes, you should help them by making them think right!

N: Is there such a thing as thinking right?

P: Yes, you will either make or mar your life depending on whether you think right or not!

N: What is the reference point? By reference to what are you talking about thinking right and thinking wrong? Are you God?

P: No, I am not God. But I am referring to God-like stuff.

N: What is that?

P: Natural laws!

N: Oh, natural laws! See, you have spent two hours so far with me for no rewards, whatsoever! You are not raising any invoice to me for your services! You are just giving your time and energy for free! Tell me which natural law is this?

P: Love!

N: Bull shit. Can I run business if I just gave my time and energy for free all the time?

P: You cannot.

N: Then what value does love have as a natural law?

P: Ask your mother.

17. Love is Love-Love

N: What will I ask her?

P: What price did she demand before feeding you?

N: See, it is quite natural.

P: What is natural?

N: Mother loving her child.

P: So, love is natural. Do you accept?

N: Yes…. love is natural. But not in business.

P: Love will make your business grow faster and better!

N: I accept all the things that you said so far. But not this. How can I practice love at workplace? Impossible.

P: Do you have anybody working for you without salary?

N: Who on earth will do that?

P: Will anyone stick to your company if you always abused him in words and deed all the time?

N: Who on earth will…?

P: So, all the employees you have basically love themselves, don't they?

N: Yes, in a way.

P: So, you have a responsibility to respect their love for themselves, right?

N: Yes.

P: Now you tell me, how did love become `bull shit' for you?

N: I am sorry. I was a little confused!

P: Even now you are!

N: What? Don't mystify. Why are you saying I am confused?

P: Assuming you respected the self-love of all the employees, and they did not acknowledge your self-love, will that be acceptable to you?

N: No.

P: Then, what works best at work-place is love-love, not any one-sided love. Only in romantic life, one-sided love is possible!

N: So, my language should ideally be, 'love for myself and love for my employees!'. But the word love is too full of overtones of compassion and forgiving. Can we not rename this natural law?

P: It has already been done! Win-win!

N: Oh, it is one and the same! But this term is non-spiritual and quite corporatist!

P: Yes, people are happy if they use jargon.

N: Is it possible always to practice win-win in work settings?

P: It is possible.

N: What if some novices are a little dull at times? Should we apply this law of win-win and terminate them simply because they are not allowing the employer to win?

P: No need, you can counsel them. You can give them some time-allowance. You can orient them towards the work. May be there is some turbulence in their personal life and they need some more time to settle down! You can train them intensely in their domain knowledge as well as life-knowledge. An untrained work-force will anytime land you in trouble.

N: What if after all the allowances their performance is not up to the mark?

P: Change their portfolio.

N: What if they fail there too?

P: Explain to them the problems you are facing in retaining them. Explain to them that their skill sets and temperament might suit another job portfolio which is not available in your company.

N: In other words, fire them?

P: That's a machine language.

N: What do you mean?

P: I have heard that only guns are fired. Not human beings.

N: What is the appropriate word, then?

P: Request for relocation (RFR)!

N: What is wrong in using the word firing when it comes to incompetent people?

P: You have no right to judge another person as competent or incompetent.

N: Why not? I have my yardstick to measure him against.

P: Do you know him fully?

N: No, I may not.

P: Did you create him?

N: What is this ridiculous question? It is God's domain to create people.

P: Then how dare you call a God's creation incompetent?

N: I am sorry. I am sorry.

P: You had better be. If a person does not suit his job profile, maybe you can call him a misfit, but never an unfit.

N: What about those hundreds of CEOs who use this term?

P: You had better mind *your* business.

N: Aren't you rude?

P: I am stern.

N: Why this sternness?

P: Mind your business.

N: Why mind my business?

P: You cannot mind others' business. You can only mind your business. You can only correct yourself. You can only change yourself.

N: Again, you are rude. I feel like....

P: Pulling your gun out? Do it if you dare.

N: Oh, now you know I am transformed. Now you know I can no longer think of gun as a solution to any problem! That's why you are teasing me!

P: Listen, don't bother who is using what language. You stick to reverential language!

N: What is this reverential language? I have associated this word only with God and godly beings. Not with ordinary human beings like my employees.

P: Then you are a conditioned puppet!

N: Again, a pejorative! Aren't you a little sadistic?

P: I am matter of fact.

N: What?

P: You are an automaton.

N: Okay, I accept you are superior and I am an automation. But tell me why you are so contemptuously calling me an automaton!

P: Because you are like a parrot.

N: What? You mean I am like you.

P: No, you are like a parrot.

N: Like you?

P: No, you are like a parrot.

N: Then what are you, if you are not a parrot?

P: You will know later.

N: When?

P: When you grow sufficiently spiritual!

N: When will that be?

P: When you make that choice!

N: I sometimes wonder if I am not wasting my time with you! You are enigmatic and a little arrogant.

P: I am matter of fact.

N: Ok, tell me why did you call me an automaton or a parrot?

P: Because you ape others!

N: Another derogatory word! Are you trying to denigrate me?

P: I am being matter of fact!

N: Hell with your matter-of-fact-ness. Now, tell me why you said I ape others.

P: Others 'fired' their employees, and you `fired' too!

N: Yes, everyone else uses that language and in order to conform I used the term, too!

P: Wasn't there a choice?

N: (Mr. Naught does not open his mouth for some time. Some internal dialogue takes place). Mr. Naught says to himself, 'Oh yes, I can exercise choice here…my choice of words is *my* choice, after all….! Let the whole world use unparliamentarily and impolite language, but I can choose to differ! Yes, I have a right!'

P: What are you muttering?

N: No, nothing! You have opened my eyes!

P: They have not been closed for some time now!

N: You are in a mood to joke. I am deeply disturbed inside. I have woken up to the truth that I have been aping others in many ways as if there had not been another choice available!

P: Don't feel bad. That's how everyone lives.

N: I am not `everyone'.

P: Are you someone special?

N: Yes, I am special and I would like to be my special self. I will treat my employees with utmost restraint and with utmost respect. My relationship with my employees is only temporary. They may suit the work or may not but they deserve respectable treatment.

P: Wow, so you are removing the word 'fire' and the four letter 'f' word from your lexicon, aren't you?

N: Yes, I feel ashamed. And I realize that I have been using this 'f' word only to cover up my own feelings of inadequacy and to maintain a false sense of superiority.

P: 'F' word is for action and not for utterance!

N: Funny! What do I do next?

P: Do it.

N: Do what?

P: This choice-making you were talking about…and it is the mark of an evolved being!

N: Why did I not know it all these years?

P: That is how life works. Ignorance comes first and knowledge comes next! The supreme human effort is to become more and more aware of the deeper and deeper levels of one's being!

N: What happens if one does not practice this self-awareness and choice-making?

P: One remains a prisoner to the limited options!

N: And I liked your perspective of seeing every human being (my employees) with dignity.

P: Such dignified treatments will not be forgotten.

N: Yes, everyone remembers only those bosses who have been more human and nourishing in their approach!

P: Such moments of nourishment will never be forgotten by the nourished although the nourisher might forget all about it.

N: Yes, it is the character of the human heart to remember the good things that it has received!

P: You are right, any more questions.

N: I have started loving and respecting you. I feel like giving a hug to you.

P: On your pants pocket you have a gun. In your heart which is one foot away from the pocket, you say you now have love! How can I trust you? If you have the capacity to allow 4 seconds to pass before making a choice between a hug and a gun, then I will have some hope!

N: Hey, that reminds me! I am told that the American President determines, proverbially, the fate of the world by holding back his decision, even under extreme provocation, for those 4 seconds before choosing the option of pushing the nuclear button. Is it true?

P: It is notional.

N: What does this indicate?

P: The responsibility of choice-making!

N: You mean to say man has to exercise responsibility when it comes to making choices, don't you?

P: Yes, an attitude of responsibility results in meaningful and sensible choices. Now, tell me, do you really want to make the choice of monopolizing all the businesses of the world?

18. A New Me

Mr, Naught thought to himself – Why should I? What drove me from inside has changed now! Yes, I love doing business. But I will not do business for the sake of doing business. Life has to be understood in its entirety. Inadequacy-driven life is not life. I will rather undertake to spread this message as part of my corporate social responsibility. And I will not encourage monopolies. Monopoly is a fool's dream! I will encourage entrepreneurship. I will campaign for empowering people in regions where there are starvation deaths. I now believe in imparting empowering information. Within three hours you have changed the course of my life. It is as if you have opened the floodgates of positivity in me. I have fallen in love with myself and the world all over again. My inner journey will continue. I will sit in non-meditation regularly. I will only listen to my inner voice. Outside factors will not govern my behavior. I really enjoyed the conversation with you.

P: Oh, you thought I could not hear your silent internal monologue? I could hear each word of it! Anyway, I am really happy for you, too!

N: Hey, Ms. Parrot! I want to ask you this – since you talk about previous births, you must also have memories of previous births, right? Tell me if we had known each other in our previous births.

P: Yes, we had known each other!

N: How? When? What were we? What were you? What was I?

P: I will let you know at the appropriate time.

N: When will that appropriate time be?

P: At the appropriate time!

N: You can drive people crazy with your answers!

Mr. Naught was just rotating and relaxing his strained neck as he had been talking for a long time to the parrot by raising his head up towards the branch of the tree where she was sitting. After a while, Mr. Naught looked up again towards the parrot and was shocked and disappointed! The parrot had already left. The moment Mr. Naught started summing up the changes that had come upon him, maybe it served as an indication for the Parrot to leave.......!

Mr. Naught to himself: 'Why did she leave all of a sudden, without a word? She said she would let me know of our past life connections. But she just flew off! Oh Ms. Parrot, will we ever get to meet again? I miss you badly!' Mr. Naught wiped the tear drops flowing down his cheeks with his handkerchief.

Mr. Naught hears someone walking towards him and he realizes it is his grandpa who was inching towards him.

Grandpa: Naught, it was strange seeing you talk to yourself for such a long time. I did not disturb you because you were in an animated dialogue with yourself!

N: No, grandpa, I was talking to a parrot that was sitting up there in that branch and she was talking to me!

Grandpa: I never heard any parrot speak. Maybe you were talking to your own conscience!

www.ingramcontent.com/pod-product-compliance
Ingram Content Group UK Ltd.
Pitfield, Milton Keynes, MK11 3LW, UK
UKHW040009200726
13854UKWH00001B/111

9 798885 916851